Dear Reader

Locations play a huge part in my stories, and for that I only have my home town of Melbourne to blame. Take this story, for example…

On the very day I planned to sit down and decide what my next book would be about I received an invitation to attend an art auction in which a friend of mine had a painting listed. It sounded like too much fun to pass up, and I wasn't disappointed. The gallery was slick and glossy, the inhabitants even more so. The prices on the artworks took my breath away. And the hushed chatter over pink champagne and catalogues created enough energy to give a girl serious goosebumps. Within five minutes there was no doubt where I would be setting my next book: Melbourne's High Street, Armadale.

High Street is a long thoroughfare, bordered by mature trees light on delicate foliage, cluttered by four-wheel drives, imported luxury cars and clattering trams, and famous for its run of graceful antiques shops and auction houses.

My darling hero, Mitch Hanover, grew from this sophisticated location without my breaking a sweat. All I had to do was throw in Veronica Bing, a flashy, exuberant, rebellious heroine, who would make the elegant people of Armadale and my Mitch stand up and take notice. My beautiful Melbourne did the rest.

If you can, do visit her one day. If you can't, I only hope my books make you feel as though you have.

Ally

www.allyblake.com

D1342702

HIRED:
THE BOSS'S BRIDE

BY
ALLY BLAKE

MILLS & BOON®
Pure reading pleasure™

First published in Great Britain 2008
Harlequin Mills & Boon Limited,
Eton House, 18-24 Paradise Road, Richmond, Surrey TW9 1SR

© Ally Blake 2008

ISBN: 978 0 263 20347 9

Set in Times Roman 10½ on 12¾ pt
07-0808-52507

Printed and bound in Great Britain
by Antony Rowe Ltd, Chippenham, Wiltshire

Having once been a professional cheerleader, **Ally Blake**'s motto is 'Smile and the world smiles with you.' One way to make Ally smile is by sending her on holidays—especially to locations which inspire her writing. New York and Italy are by far her favourite destinations. Other things that make her smile are the gracious city of Melbourne, the gritty Collingwood football team, and her gorgeous husband Mark

Reading romance novels was a smile-worthy pursuit from long back. So, with such valuable preparation already behind her, she wrote and sold her first book. Her career as a writer also gives her a perfectly reasonable excuse to indulge in her stationery addiction. That alone is enough to keep her grinning every day!

Ally would love you to visit her at her website www.allyblake.com

Ally Blake also writes for Modern Heat™!

Recent books by the same author:

FALLING FOR THE REBEL HEIR
  (Romance)
THE MAGNATE'S INDECENT PROPOSAL
  (Modern Heat™)

I wholeheartedly dedicate this tome to
Mark, Leon, Beverley, Susan, Leith, Dennis and Alli,
without whom my gorgeous little girl
might never have brightened my world.

CHAPTER ONE

WHEN Veronica Bing was a little girl, her grand plan in life was to have blue eyes and blonde hair.

Long blonde hair down to her waist and the kind of baby-blue eyes that made a girl able to get away with anything. And to be a fairy princess with wings. And braces on her teeth and divorced parents as all the kids at school had them. Oh, and she'd wanted a hot-pink car.

Not too much to ask, right?

Instead, her hair had grown thick, wavy and dark, and after six months in her late teens, when she'd fulfilled her lifelong dream of being blonde, she'd realised she'd looked like a fruit-cake and gone back to her natural brunette. Alas her eyes had also remained muddy brown from shortly after she was born and she'd had to learn to find other ways to get what she wanted.

The wings had never appeared. In fact, she'd soon discovered she was allergic to flying—if nausea, sweating palms and short-ness of breath could be classed as signs of an allergy. Funnily enough mangoes, apricots and tall, dark handsome men who saw her as the answer to all their connubial dreams produced the same symptoms. Hence the fact that she as yet remained prince-free, making the princess dream also null and void.

Her teeth had grown spectacularly well, unfortunately without help of braces. And as she'd been a happy accident, a late and only child of Don and Phyllis Bing who'd been about to hit their fifties at the time she was born and by that stage had been married thirty years already, her parents had never divorced. Instead her father had died of a heart attack while Veronica was still in high school and her mother had taken her time passing away from a broken heart. Though the medicos had claimed it was Alzheimer's, Veronica had left university to care for her mum and thus knew better.

And as to the hot-pink car? Well, one out of seven wasn't bad!

Cruising the backstreets of inner-east Melbourne in her very hot, very pink, very expensive-to-maintain Corvette, Veronica slipped down a gear, slowed, pushed her sunglasses onto her forehead, and made sure she was in the right place before curving neatly and noisily onto High Street, Armadale.

Her hair flapped about her ears as she trundled at a snail's pace behind a tram. Together they passed historic shopfronts, antique stores, up-market boutiques and art galleries nestled comfortably next to one another along the elegant oak-lined street. Four-wheel drives lined up nose to tail with German-made luxury cars and the people stepping in and out of them all looked as if they'd just come from the salon via a shopping trip in Milan.

'You're not on the Gold Coast any more, Ms Bing,' Veronica said out loud, before sliding her sunglasses back into place.

The tram creaked to a stop, and so did her Corvette. Veronica let her head fall against the headrest and looked up into the bright blue sky. A web of tram cables glittered over her head and she had to blink against the bright sunlight flickering through the wide gaps.

She sniffed deep, letting the sights and sounds of Melbourne, the town in which she'd been born, come back to her after a good six years away. She wondered how it would treat her return: with wide-open arms, or with a cliquish turn of its graceful head?

She hoped the former because the job she was in town to interview for—in-house auctioneer for an established and esteemed art gallery—sounded just perfect. It was temporary, it was immediate and it meant working with a close friend she hadn't seen in yonks. And *super* especially it was located at the other end of the country from her last job. And thus her last boss.

Thoughts of her dash from Queensland with nothing but a suitcase and her car and the exultant resignation message she'd left on Geoffrey's answering machine, made her next breath in a tad shaky. But not because she was worried; because she was free.

So what if she was jobless and homeless? So what if this job opportunity Kristin had mentioned in passing on the phone the week prior was the only opportunity currently on her horizon? So what if her next car payment was due in less than a week and her bank balance was laughable?

She caught her reflection in the rear-vision mirror and checked her lipstick. 'No pressure,' she said, a wry smile tugging at the corner of her mouth.

The tram heaved to a start. Veronica saw her chance to slip past while the cumbersome trolley slowly got up to speed, then she purred off down the road on the lookout for what Kristin had described as a two-storey, redbrick building, the façade of which was reminiscent of an old fire station. The Hanover House Art and Antique Gallery.

Mitch Hanover paced behind the oversized reception desk of stately Hanover House, the enduring antique and art auction business his family had owned for generations.

'So what is the time?' his assistant, Kristin, asked.

He looked up from the watch he'd been staring at for the past thirty-odd seconds and stared through the large arched front windows to the street outside. 'It's late. *She's* late. I thought you told me this friend of yours was a pro.'

Kristin angled her hip against the edge of the desk and glowered at him. 'I said she was the answer to all your dreams. If you saw "pro" in that, then who am I to argue?'

He growled at the back of his throat, and then gave up when he remembered who he was talking to. 'You do realise she's my last interview, do you not? We are going to have to choose a new auctioneer by the end of today or next week's pre-show will have to be cancelled.'

He didn't need to add that if the pre-show was cancelled, the show itself would soon follow. And after that would fall the business itself. Everyone in the building knew it. Knew it, dreaded it, yet somehow expected it.

Kristin, imperturbable as always, grinned. 'Don't panic, Mitch. She's perfect. So perfect that within the hour you'll be eating humble pie. You just wait and see.'

He narrowed his eyes, his hogwash radar prickling feverishly in the back of his head until it resulted in a headache.

Trying to distract himself, he picked up and began playing with an ancient fountain pen that looked as if it had seen better days. Better centuries, in fact. Why people liked collecting relics of the past, he had no idea. The future was his game.

He put the pen back where he found it.

'And stop frowning,' Kristin said. 'Unfair as it is on the whole men age far better than women but that doesn't mean you want to hurry the process.'

'Has it ever occurred to you that I only frown when you're in the room?'

'Never. You need a massage. Or a week off. Ever been camping? Communing with nature can be very relaxing. No? Then how about dinner with someone who can string a sentence together without prefacing every other word with an "um". Serial-dating walking clichés will age you even more than frowning overly much ever could. I read that somewhere recently.'

'Maybe you're the one who ought to be looking for a new job,' he said with the kind of humourless smile that usually sent his minions running to their desks in fear.

Kristin merely blinked. 'Why on earth would I do that?'

Mitch gave up and ran a hand over his forehead, surprised to find just how deep the furrows in fact were. 'When's my next appointment in the city?'

Kristin poked at some buttons on her BlackBerry. Her eyes widened a tad, but when she looked back to him she was the picture of innocence. 'You have plenty of time. Relax.'

Relax? As if he could relax. He'd been blithe for far too long, spending years in London greedily gobbling up emerging markets, IT and telecommunications companies into the Hanover Enterprises fold and all the while Hanover House, the one-time jewel in the crown of the Hanover family business, the business his parents had poured their hearts and souls into before retirement, had been run deep into the ground by lax and old-fashioned management.

He felt the imminent failure of the foundation business like a heavy weight upon his already overloaded shoulders. Now he was back, now he had nothing tying him to London anymore, now he was CEO of Hanover Enterprises, he couldn't relax while something his parents loved so dearly upped and died.

The growl of a high-end sports car split the taut silence and he glanced up to see a hot-pink Corvette slip into a tiny no-parking space right in front of the gallery.

'Idiot,' he said beneath his breath, the expulsion of the word relieving his stress a little bit. The council was so hot in this part of town the guy'd be towed within the hour. He knew well enough. It had happened to him twice.

The engine cut off, leaving the blare of some awful eighties party track pulsating through the gallery windows before that too shut off, leaving the room filled with its usual musty silence.

Kristin suddenly made an excited squeak and pushed past him as she ran outside. She hit the Corvette and leant in so far to hug the occupant her feet came off the ground and Mitch had to avert his gaze so as not to see if her stockings were full or held up by suspenders.

Then it hit him. The idiot driver had to be Veronica Bing. His final interview. Naturally. It was some time since he'd decided God enjoyed punishing him. And longer still since he'd known why. His brow-furrowing hit epic proportions.

He took in a deep breath. He'd interview the woman, he'd hire one of the three other perfectly adequate candidates and then he'd take delight in informing Kristin her Christmas bonus this year was going to be a canned ham.

Once Kristin's feet fluttered back to the ground Mitch moved so that he could get a better look at the kind of person Kristin—a woman he'd until this moment trusted with his Christmas shopping, his travel packing and with ordering just the right kind of flowers with which to say 'it's been lovely knowing you but…' —supposed might be the answer to all his dreams.

The answer was tall with dark brown curls and even darker huge sunglasses covering half her face, beneath which surprisingly lush red lips stretched out into a shiny white smile. He made out the flash of a sleeveless black T-shirt, which revealed a pair of long, lean arms that had been kissed by a far kinder sun than seen in Melbourne over the long winter. And when Kristin shook her hard before enveloping her in another hug, he could all but hear the dozen odd black bangles on her left wrist rattling.

Not bothering to open the door of the low-slung car, she of the red lips vaulted over the side and the soles of her boots came to a loud slap on the pavement. Black, they were, and knee high. With the tightest pair of dark denim jeans Mitch had ever seen tucked into them. Jeans that encased the kind of curves that would make any half-alive man sit up and pay attention.

Mitch cricked his neck. He was at least half alive, and when he'd woken up that morning, he'd had no intention of paying such close attention to any woman, much less one he might well be about to hire. But his eyes were riveted to the creature on the other side of the glass.

He pulled at the Windsor knot of his tie, which suddenly felt too tight. It wasn't. He'd been tying that exact knot since his first day of private prep school when he was five years old. That morning he'd also woken at five on the dot as he always did. He'd taken his usual five kilometre run on the treadmill in his apartment. He'd eaten his usual low GI, high-fibre breakfast.

Usually that austere routine was enough to allay midday surges of adrenalin at nothing more than the sight of a nice backside in a pair of tight jeans. He blamed Kristin with all that talk of nature and massages and dating women with lingual skills. She'd talked him into feeling this way, thinking this way. And he would simply have to talk himself out of it.

The future of the business is in your hands, he reminded himself. *This is not the time for a momentary lapse in judgement*. He also consoled himself with the fact Veronica Bing was wearing the least likely interview outfit he could have imagined and therefore couldn't possibly be what he, or the business, needed in order to move forward. Hadn't the woman heard of a navy suit and beige stockings?

Then when his interviewee bent into the car, kicking one long leg behind her as she reached into the back seat to pull out a large silver handbag, he gave himself one last chance in hell of pulling himself together by closing his eyes and turning away.

The bell over the double oak doors clanged. Mitch opened his eyes, drew in a breath, looked straight down the barrel of the respectful portrait of his great-grandfather, Phineas Hanover, which hung behind the reception desk, muttered, 'Heaven help me,' then turned to the bright windows.

And in she came, bringing with her a waft of warm spring air and raucous conversation as Kristin prattled on beside her like an overexcited teenager.

He readied himself to take the proceedings in hand but his words stopped in his mouth when he caught a load of the image emblazoned across Veronica's T-shirt. A huge pair of glistening red lips followed the dips and curves of her chest.

The ensuing tightness in Mitch's chest was definitely not the result of hyperventilation. Or a stitch, as he hadn't made a move. And it couldn't be a heart attack. He was thirty-four and fit as a fiddle, for Pete's sake.

He blinked, breathed deep and looked up into her eyes instead. Only to find that without the huge sunglasses covering half her face she was...*lovely*. There was no other word that he could bring to mind no matter how hard he tried. With all that tousled dark hair that made her look as if she'd just rolled out of bed, a pair of sparkling dark eyes and skin so tanned and healthy-looking she practically shone.

Mitch felt the faint but conspicuous beginnings of a chemical reaction deep within his bones before it quickly spread, making his palms tingle and the hairs on the back of his neck stand on end. Saying the rapid rush of such a feeling shocked the hell out of him would have been an understatement.

When Veronica's eyes finally swung from Kristin's beaming face to look his way, he actually braced himself for impact.

Her smile faltered. Even from that distance, and with the sun behind her, he saw it. Felt it. Then her gaze raked him from the top of his dark hair, down his conservative suit to his freshly shone shoes and back to his eyes again. And his skin contracted as though it had been one long red fingernail that had traced his skin rather than the casual caress of a pair of big brown female eyes.

She broke eye contact and the skin on the back of his neck suddenly felt cold, as though he'd come out in a sweat. Which was ridiculous. This whole thing was quite simply all too ridiculous. He was a man of experience. Far wider reaching experience than he would admit to in polite company. And in his experience he'd come to believe that this kind of instantaneous, primal, physical reaction to a woman was no longer his to be had. The fact that he'd cultivated his indifference to the point of it being an art form all of itself was beside the point.

He ran a hand up the back of his neck and tried to remember the last time he'd eaten.

Out of the corner of his eye he saw Veronica pat Kristin on the shoulder and ask her something that had them both looking his way.

'Right,' Kristin said, shaking her head. 'I'd forgotten all about him.'

Way to build me up as the dominant player in this here situation, Mitch thought.

He shot Kristin a look that had her biting her lip, then he turned his attentions back to the newcomer. He reminded his professional self how much he needed an interim stopgap to save the family business. He informed his personal self that this interloper was the *exact* antithesis of the kind of cool, cavalier blondes who usually caught his eye. While in the back of his head Kristin's voice told him she was the answer to all his dreams.

'Mitch Hanover,' he said, walking the final two steps towards her. He held out a hand. 'You must be Veronica Bing.'

'What gave it away?' she asked, taking his hand and shaking. Hard, sharp, determined, like a man. But at the same time she gave a saucy little curtsy, one foot tucked neatly behind the other as she bowed her head with respect.

He slid his hand away; slow enough it wouldn't draw suspicion, fast enough he wouldn't have to put up with any superfluous lingering memory of her touch upon his skin.

'The other three interviewees didn't object when I offered them plane tickets to come here,' he said, glancing past her at her ostentatious car. 'Return plane tickets.'

One thin dark eyebrow shot skyward, and her tongue darted out to moisten her full lower lip. 'It seems my irrational fear of flying has given me an edge over my competition. I knew one day it would come in handy.'

Her mouth curved into a slight smile. He felt his own tug at the corners. He caught himself just in time.

'I'm sure Kristin has informed you of the importance and immediacy we have placed on the auctioneer role. We have a massive new show set to kick off next week, no auctioneer in place and half the staff down with the flu.' Though Mitch thought it more likely that they figured, in most cases correctly, if they came back in, they'd be sacked on the spot. 'The very future of this business depends on filling this position with exactly the right person.'

At this point the other three interviewees had respectively

been sanctimonious, blasé and terrified. Veronica Bing, on the other hand, grinned.

'Well, now, that's the most unappealing sales pitch I've ever heard. Mitch Hanover, I do believe you need me more than you even realise.'

Her bold words hung between them like a bright, shiny red apple: tempting as all get out, and just as likely to be poisoned as not.

He inwardly cursed the last inept auctioneer who'd brought the place to its knees with his lackadaisical ways, the doddery old curator for having no clue about current market trends and his parents for being so good to him he couldn't let them down.

But he was here now. And so was Veronica Bing. He might as well get it over with.

'Why don't you head on through the gallery and I'll join you in a moment?' he asked, waving a hand in the direction of the rear office.

'Whatever you say, boss.' She swanned across the shiny grey carpet of the wide-open lobby and up the polished wood stairs and disappeared behind the huge brick partition hiding the gallery itself from the road view.

'Isn't she something?' Kristin asked from behind him.

Mitch sucked his breath in through his teeth. 'She's something, all right. I'm just not quite sure what.'

Veronica took the moment to herself to try to stop her knees from shaking.

'So far so good,' she whispered to herself. 'You're doing fine. Chin up, back straight, look him in the eye and wow him with your confidence.'

Confidence? Ha! She could barely remember what the word meant. A week ago this move had sounded so fantastic by the light of a message machine that had been blinking with a dozen messages left by a man who didn't seem to understand the word '*No*'.

But now, here, in this big, old, musty, gilded building that echoed with the cultured voices of people who'd walked in her shoes, she felt more than a little intimidated.

The grey papered walls were faded, the massive chandelier in the middle of the entrance looked as if it hadn't worked in a century and the gunk on the walls, gilded frames around pictures of fussy-looking, overfed royalty, what she could only assume was supposed to be art, were so far beyond her taste and life experience as to seem alien.

Then there was Kristin, the girl who'd once had more piercings than Veronica had handbags, now with a slick dark bob and dressed in an elegant beige trouser suit, while she'd trundled up in her tight jeans and knee-high boots and T-shirt, the exact kind of thing she'd worn to work every day in her last post, auctioning patents on computer-game intellectual property.

She bit back a groan as she imagined throwing herself on the bonnet of her beloved Corvette while it was taken away by goons hired by her bank.

She glanced back over her shoulder. Whatever predicament she had landed herself in, the answer came down to Mitch Hanover; the man who had her future in his firm, long-fingered hands.

Kristin had called him a slave-driving stuffed shirt on more than one occasion. Veronica had thus pictured a balding, over-fed, pompous, pasty, married guy on daily blood-pressure medication. Compared with her last boss, the personable, clean-cut and ultimately indiscreet Geoffrey, that combination of traits had sounded like her salvation.

Salvation, as it turned out, had been offered to her in the form of a man whose dark grey suit, darker tie and crisp pinstriped shirt were pressed to the point of agony. But it was the stuff stuffed inside the shirt that made the bigger impact.

Mitch Hanover was beautiful. The kind of beautiful a young girl with dreams of princes and fairy wings and all that jazz would go weak at the knees for.

A shade over thirty, a bit more over six feet tall, with matinee-idol looks, an assemblage of dark preppy hair, sharp jaw and per-suasively curved mouth. Stuck in a room with a young Cary Grant and Paul Newman he would have held his own.

But the things that had hit her first, last and every moment in between were his eyes. He had the kind of deep grey eyes that gave her the feeling it wouldn't take all that much to make them sparkle.

Unfortunately she hadn't managed it. Yet. But since he hadn't turned her on her heel and sent her packing, she had time. All for the sake of getting the job, of course. That was why she'd come home. Not to ogle, or allow herself to be consistently ogled, by a colleague. Supremely ogle-worthy though he might well be.

Downstairs Kristin began whispering to her boss animatedly, arms flailing, going pink in the face, no doubt talking her up, while Mitch remained cool, aloof, unflappable. It didn't ease Veronica's mind any.

In fact, watching him standing there surrounded by all that gilded finery, his fine mouth pressed into a straight line, his eyes unreadable, his whole mien making him seem as if he took life far too seriously, he made her feel distinctly nervous. Little but-terflies came to life in her stomach and she slid a hand beneath her T-shirt and tried her best to silently talk them down.

As though he knew he was being watched Mitch chose that exact moment to glance up at her, his intense grey eyes send-ing the tummy butterflies into hysterics.

Car payments, car payments, car payments, she repeated inside her head.

She slid her hand from her tummy and casually waved it at a random picture on the wall, some great hulking green monstrosity that looked as if it had been painted by a blindfolded monkey. She poked out her bottom lip and nodded, feigning great appreciation.

Mitch's gaze trailed away, lingered for a moment on the painting, then shifted back to her. From that distance she could have sworn his eyebrows raised a very little, and that his already enticing mouth turned upwards into the lightest of wry smiles, as though he wasn't of the mind to take the thing home and stick it on his wall, either.

But then he blinked and once again became a wall of poised professionalism. *Shame*, she thought. When he let his latent charm shine on through she thought he had great potential for fun.

She cleared her throat and reiterated the new grand plan she had come up with once she'd realised how ridiculous the Barbie hair, wings and fairy-dust ambitions really were: *Be good. Work hard. Take care of you. Eat more greens.* So long as she stuck to those rules, surely her life would change for the better.

Mitch barked some instructions at Kristin, who nodded and was on the phone sounding professional and brisk in an instant, before he jogged up the stairs to arrive at Veronica's side. He brought with him a flutter of subtly sexy aftershave that had her breathing deep through her nose, then mentally berating herself for being so weak.

'Whatever Kristin's been telling you about me,' she said, 'believe about half.'

'But which half would I choose?' He glanced sideways at her as he strode past and her knees began to shake all over again.

She jogged to catch up. 'Whichever fools you into thinking that, beneath this ravishing style icon before you, I'm actually more like you than you're thinking; I'm sophisticated, responsible, meticulous, fair and open to new ideas and challenges.'

'Now, what makes you think I am any one of those things, Ms Bing?'

'Eternal optimism?' she tried.

He kept walking a step ahead of her, but this time she sensed the wry smile for sure.

The butterflies calmed down to a mild buzz, and Veronica felt herself edge a step closer towards landing the job. To truly starting afresh.

And this time she wouldn't screw it all up.

Mitch didn't slow until he'd reached the back office, though Veronica Bing and her long legs, warm persuasive scent and effervescent babbling kept up just fine.

'Do you mind if I use your office, Boris?' he asked the curator who had been around the place since before he could remember. 'I have another interview to conduct.'

Boris eyed him warily, as did most of the gallery staff whenever he deigned to set foot in the place. Nevertheless the older man was enough of a gentleman to acquiesce. 'Of course, young sir.'

After dragging a high-backed, ornately carved antique chair around for Veronica to sit upon, Mitch swung to the commanding side of the desk.

He sat, and looked up to see that Veronica had ignored the offer of a seat. Instead, as Boris passed she reached out and ran a finger and a thumb over the curl of his red bow tie. 'Very debonair.'

Boris blushed. He honest to goodness blushed.

sure he'd ever even seen the fellow smile, much less find enough raw emotion within himself to blush. He was beginning to fear that the woman might well be some kind of witch.

'Why, thank you,' Boris finally managed to spit out when he found his tongue again. 'Good luck, miss.'

And was his back actually straighter as he shuffled out into the gallery?

Mitch sat back and pondered the situation at hand. If this woman could have both he and old Boris gobsmacked within seconds of meeting her, he wondered just what she might be able to do with a roomful of red-hot Armadale art collectors. Would she outshine them all or would they eat her alive?

'So who's Boris when he's at home?' Veronica asked as she sauntered around the cluttered room, picking up lovingly polished *objets d'art*, turning them over, sniffing one or two, then putting them back on whatever spare space she could find. Mitch could only hope they hadn't been placed in any particular order, or that at least they'd been catalogued and photographed already.

He swung back in the chair and crossed his right ankle over his left knee. 'Boris is the gallery's curator and currently the senior employee.'

'He runs the joint? So why isn't he interviewing me?'

For want of a clearer way to draw the line as to just who was in charge here, in the business and in the interview, Mitch said, 'Because I *own* the joint.'

She stopped her perusal and her gaze swung back to his, dark and bright all at once. And those lips of hers, slices of luscious red, curved upwards into the kind of smile any warm-blooded man could not for the life of him ignore.

Lucky for him it had been some time since his blood had run higher than lukewarm.

He silently cleared his throat and told himself that saucy smile meant she was not in the least bit awed by him and his hiring and firing rights, which wasn't a good start to the proceedings, or any kind of working relationship.

'Take a seat, Ms Bing,' he insisted in his most sober boss-like voice.

She dropped her sleek form into a chair and crossed one long leg over the other and said, 'Of course, Mr Hanover.'

Was she mocking him? Seriously? From nowhere a bubble of stunned laughter rose into Mitch's throat. He swallowed it down before it took any kind of hold.

Then his voice dropped a good three notes as he produced his most officious glower and said, 'Now would be a good time to show me your résumé.'

She shook her head. 'No résumé.'

'No résumé?'

'When has a résumé ever told you anything about a prospective employee more valuable than the things you discovered simply by talking?'

He opened his mouth to deny it, but she made a fair point. One he'd always believed in, hence the reason he was here now rather than some overtrained human resources lackey. 'Okay, so then why don't you tell me a bit about your experience?'

When her smile shifted sideways, lifting one rosy cheek until a sincerely adorable dimple appeared, Mitch shifted in his chair and wished this day over.

'Your experience in the auctioneering field,' he qualified.

'Right.' She smiled at him some more, lots and lots of goodness knew what going on behind those bright brown eyes. Then she leant forward, her fingers with their blood-red nails gripping the edge of the desk. 'Is this really going to be one of *those* interviews? Where you ask for my references and I have to come up with some sham, off-the-cuff answer to "What's your worst flaw?"?'

Mitch could do little but stare.

The other interviews had taken around twenty minutes a piece, the well-qualified participants answering exactly *those* sorts of questions without complaint. In fact, they'd answered them with great preparation and poise. And he was a busy man with other pressing projects to ably fill any spare time he might have. Back in the city in his nice big office behind a nice big door manned by a Rottweiler of a receptionist whom he would have trusted to take a bullet for him rather than expect him to deal with the kind of frivolity he was dealing with right now.

He too sat forward. 'Would it be a huge problem for you if it were *that* kind of interview? We can end this now if that's the case.'

Maybe that would be for the best, he thought. Despite the growing desire to see what throwing a firecracker like her into a place like this might achieve. For then she and her long legs and bright eyes and hot lips and crazy car would be gone from the fringe of his life. As would the sense that she would end up being more trouble than she was worth.

But instead of giving in and admitting they were obviously a bad fit, she smiled more, wider. And the sense that he was no more in charge of this interview than the chair beneath his backside grew stronger than ever.

'Mr Hanover,' she said, 'Mitch. All you need to know is I'm it. I'm your girl. I'm the best you're ever going to meet. This job you are looking to fill isn't about an extensive knowledge of those old paintings out there. It isn't about who I know, or where I've come from. Auctioneering is about selling people what they already think they need: land, lifestyle, dreams, the next big idea, golden trinkets. The product doesn't matter. What matters is the pleasure I can gift your clients when they buy from you. As it is *that* pleasure that will become their lasting memory of dealing with Hanover House.'

She finished off her speech with a grin. And Mitch realised all too late that the strange tugging feeling around the edges of his face was the result of him actually smiling back. The soothing lilt of her voice, her utter conviction, the way she un-flinchingly held his eyes with hers… Hell, if she'd tried to resell him the building beneath his feet he had a feeling he might have asked how much.

He slowly relaxed until he was back in control of his facial features, then sat back, rubbing a finger along the dip beneath his bottom lip while he let the idea of her trickle through his flinty outer shell.

She was sassy. Confident. And, despite her apparent lack of regard for form and tradition, she was selling herself like crazy. She wasn't here on a whim. She really wanted the job. And he really, *really* needed someone to do it. Someone who actually had a chance of bringing the business into the twenty-first century. And quick smart.

He thought back to the portrait of his great-grandfather, the founder of Hanover House, hanging imposingly over the recep-tion desk. He wondered what old Phineas would have made of Ms Tight Pants. If the guy had had a pittance of the Hanover charm he was famous for, Mitch was pretty sure the crusty old goat would have been smitten.

He asked, 'And you don't have any qualms about selling people things they don't need?'

'They're grown-ups, right? Let them do as they please with their money. If they want to blow it all on red at the casino, on drought relief in Africa or on a shiny big ring for their mistress, then who are we to stop them?'

Mitch scratched his head. Who was this woman and where had she come from? 'I wouldn't have pegged you for a cynic, Ms Bing.'

She was all blinking dark lashes and radiant smiles as she said, 'And why ever not?'

Fifteen minutes later Mitch once again stood in the foyer, watching Veronica Bing and her tight denim and bouncy dark curls walk away.

The woman is a walking mantrap, he thought, hands in his trouser pockets as he tugged at the hairs on his thighs in punishment for allowing his eyes to remain focussed just south of her beltline.

She spun suddenly, walking backwards, and his eyes zoomed north. 'See you tomorrow, boss!'

'Not me,' he said, somewhat relieved for it to be the truth. 'Boris will show you the ropes from here.'

Her pace didn't falter, though he could have sworn her smile dropped. But with the sun in his eyes it might well have been all in his imagination, which had been acting as though it were on some kind of stimulant ever since she'd walked through his door.

'And there I was,' she said, 'thinking I'd be spending tomorrow strapped to a chair, toothpicks keeping my eyelids open, while you trained me in the ways of the Hanover business principles using graphs and pie charts and ancient battle cries.'

Mitch again felt a smile tug at the corners of his mouth, but since she was on her way out the door, he let it happen. 'That's week two.'

She smiled in return, and that time he knew it wasn't his imagination, because he felt it clear across the room. He balled his hands into fists until his nails dug sharply into his palms.

She waved. He nodded. And then she was out the door.

The six-week contract he'd half had in mind for the position had been stretched out to six months, for how could she be expected to move cities for less time than any sane landlord would offer on an apartment lease? How indeed. Though the clothing, petrol and moving allowances she'd initially insisted she could not live without had been summarily refused, the fluid working hours, a refurbishment budget and carte blanche to run the auctions the way she saw fit had made it through the hashing-out process.

Mitch consoled himself with the fact that he was on such a tight time limit that, if she'd held strong on some of her other requests, he might well have given in to them, as well. Grudgingly. And at least now the deal was done and the toughest little negotiator he'd come across in some time was on his side forthwith.

As he watched Veronica toss her shiny silver handbag into the seat of her audacious pink car a parking inspector sauntered up, notebook open. A malevolent kind of thrill shot through him, much like the feeling of anticipation that came just before a champ was knocked out in a title fight.

'This'll be good,' he said to nobody in particular, leaning against the desk to get the best view possible for when she was taught a much-needed lesson in supremacy and command.

Veronica sidled up to the man in blue, smiling and leaning to look over his shoulder. Mitch remembered then the way she'd smelled when she'd leant in to shake on the employment deal: exotic and fresh all at once. How her dark eyes had seemed lit from within as she'd put across her point of view. How charming was her lopsided smile.

The parking inspector didn't stand a chance.

It was barely a moment later that the guy glanced her way, laughed and tore up the sheet in his hand. Veronica took the torn-up pieces of paper, tucked them down her top, gave him a pat on the arm, jumped into her ridiculous car, revved the engine with enough va-va-voom every other retailer within spitting distance no doubt had their noses to the front windows of their shops and, with a flick of her riotous dark curls, off she zoomed.

CHAPTER TWO

'YOU coming, Mitch?' Kristin asked.

Mitch watched distractedly as Kristin felt around with her feet until she found her heels beneath the guest chair in his office and slipped them back on.

He'd known a woman once who had made a habit of the exact same move; her eyes devouring the Sunday papers, her mouth focussed on downing the last of her tea, while her feet worked unconsciously beneath her chair preparing to whisk her off to the library for hours of research for the doctorate she'd never finished.

'Mitch?' Kristin said, and he slid back to the present.

He rubbed a quick rough hand over his face as he asked, 'Am I coming where exactly?'

Kristin stood, hoisted her handbag over her shoulder and rolled her eyes. 'To the welcome Veronica drinks. I've only mentioned it a thousand times over the past few days.'

So she had. Enough that he hadn't been able to go a day without thinking about his new employee. Wondering if she'd found a place to live. If she'd bought herself an outfit more appropriate for her new position or if she'd turned up to work at Hanover House in an array of tight trousers and suggestive T-shirts. If he'd done exactly the wrong thing in hiring her because she might be just radical enough to finally run the place into the ground all on her lonesome.

'Come,' Kristin begged when he didn't instantly say his usual *no*. 'Do. Everyone from the gallery will be there, as will a whole bunch from the office who overheard the words "Friday-night happy hour" and invited themselves. I'm sure it would do them all a load of good to see the Big Boss knows how to let his hair down too.'

Mitch ran a quick hand over his short back and sides haircut, which had never been more than a centimetre longer than it was now, even while at university. 'You go. I still have too much to do here,' he said, even though Kristin held his life in her BlackBerry and knew exactly how up to date and organised he always was.

'You could always ask Manda to come,' she said, cocking a hip and not looking as if she was heading out his door anytime soon.

'Could I, now?'

'Mmm-hmm.'

As if that weren't enough reason for him to stay away. He and the accounts junior from Jefferson Corp two floors down had had three dates. One more and she'd start asking more of him than he was prepared to give. And he'd learnt three years and more blondes ago that three dates was exactly the precise cut-off point where they wouldn't get hurt and he couldn't get caught.

'Unless this would make it date four, then you'd better stay away,' Kristin said, tapping a finger against her lips as she counted back. 'I'm thinking pale pink tulips to break it off with this one.'

He slanted his eyes her way. 'You're a regular laugh riot, you are.'

She grinned, and stood waiting in the doorway of his office. 'So does that mean you're coming?'

He threw his fountain pen onto his desk and wondered exactly what Veronica Bing might choose to wear for Friday-night drinks if her interview outfit ran to knee-high boots and tight jeans. Somehow, compared with the lack of nutrition in his fridge at home and given the unusual empty space in his after-hours appointments diary, it seemed too interesting a prospect to miss.

'You convinced me.' He stood and grabbed his suit jacket from the back of his chair. 'Though if anybody gets too drunk, I'm not going to be the one dropping them home. And don't invite Manda.'

'Deal,' Kristin said, practically skipping as she led him out of the office.

Veronica sipped a Bloody Mary as she watched Mitch Hanover smile and nod at a young, cute, skinny blonde draped all over him at the bar.

He'd been true to his word. She hadn't seen or heard from him once in the days since the interview. Which was a good thing, really, especially when she'd been reminded on a daily basis since why getting too friendly with the boss was a bad, bad thing.

While finding an apartment that would accept a six-month lease, getting to know the Hanover House staff and frequenting the local hardware store to find some bargains for the changes she wanted to make to the gallery, she'd also had to deal with phone call after phone call from a bewildered Geoffrey, who as it turned out had taken her leaving far worse than she'd imagined he would.

As it turned out he'd been about to offer her a key to his apartment. A key! Which wasn't as petrifying as a ring, but still ridiculous considering they'd had two and a half dates in as many months. Ridiculous, but unfortunately not all that shocking.

The great curse of her life was that the time she had spent looking after her sick mum had left a lasting impression upon her. A kind of Florence Nightingale tinge that she couldn't seem to wash away. No matter how hard she tried to stifle it so that she could get on with becoming a successful, sought-after, self-confident businesswoman with space of her own, with a job that both broadened her limited horizons and absorbed her, her ambitions had again and again been smothered by men who missed all that and only saw a soft, mushy, empathetic shoulder to lean on.

Explaining all that to Geoffrey had been pointless. There'd been tears, there'd been tantrums, there'd been the sound of ceramics smashing on the floor, and none of that had been from her end.

A high-pitched giggle tugged her from her reverie and back to the long mahogany bar, glossy and shimmering with the reflected light of a half-dozen funky cone-shaped lamps above. Blondie was still there doing her all to show Mitch Hanover she could be soft, mushy and empathetic for him and much, much more.

Blondie giggled loudly again and it screeched down Veronica's nerves like fingernails down a blackboard. Mitch didn't seem to mind in the least.

Men...

Today this man wore another dark suit, a different pale pinstriped shirt and an ever-so-slightly more frivolous tie—it was embroidered. The tailored clothing made him look far too intense for her comfort, yet at the same time she still found him remarkably yummy.

Especially when comparing him with the men of her recent acquaintance. Gold Coast men wore relaxed linen, bright ties, and none of them could remember the original colour of their teeth. Whereas Mitch Hanover was straight, intense, dark and self-contained. It was like comparing used-car salesmen with a Master of the Universe and she couldn't deny she instinctively preferred the latter sort a heck of a lot more.

Perhaps it was the fact that he didn't look like the kind of guy who needed a shoulder to lean on. His shoulders seemed plenty broad enough to handle a whole world of troubles and then some.

'He never comes,' Kristin whispered into her ear.

'Who never what?' Veronica asked, dragging her eyes away quick smart for fear she'd been caught staring.

'Our venerable boss,' Kristin said. 'He never comes to these social things.'

'Never?' Veronica asked, turning straight back to gaze his way now she had a good excuse to do so.

'Not once,' Kristin said while sipping at her mixed drink through a skinny pink straw. 'This is a total first.'

'Maybe he didn't have plans tonight.'

'Maybe. Though it looks to me as if he's busy making them.'

Veronica experienced a rapid tightness in her chest at the thought. It felt a whole lot like envy. Which was an unforgivable reaction considering Geoffrey had been promoted while she'd had to move cities, change jobs and listen to him whinge about how she had put him out.

She turned away from the bar for good this time and pointed to a set of deep cream tub chairs in the corner of the plush carpeted room. 'So how about you and Mitch?'

'Me and Mitch what?' Kristin asked, sitting, then bopping on her seat along with the Elvis classic purring from the tastefully hidden speakers scattered about the opulent room.

'Have you ever been...*on*?'

'On what?'

Veronica rolled her eyes. '*On*. You know...*together*. We spend so many hours with those we work with it's only natural to gravitate towards one another.'

Natural, she thought. *That sounds way better than a pathological case of repeatedly mistaking the man in charge as a man in charge of his own life.*

Kristin choked on her drink. 'Me? And Mitch? Mitch Hanover? A-blonde-a-minute Mitch Hanover? My boss? The man who pays my very nice wages? And lets me take Thursday afternoons off for a manicure and pedicure as thanks for the long hours I put in?'

Veronica noticed she hadn't actually answered the question. 'You don't think he's cute?'

'Of course I think he's cute,' Kristin said, without even a pause. Then she glanced at Mitch, who was now alone at the bar, talking into his mobile phone with a frown on his face. She took another sip, then looked thoughtfully back at her friend. 'To tell you the truth, if he'd asked early on I wouldn't have said no. It's just...you see he has this particular thing for blondes. Fun and frivolous blondes. Much younger blondes. The kind who wouldn't know a da Vinci from a Rossetti. Which could be dead dreary and predictable coming from another man, but for our Mitch it's understandable, really. Considering...'

Kristin's words trailed off into an expressive sigh.

Veronica couldn't for the life of her think why being a gorgeous hotshot gave a man an excuse not to date women of his own generation. In fact, she found herself taking it somewhat personally. 'How young?'

'Zygotes. Truly. Wrinkle-free ones for whom *gravity* was a word they heard at school, not a physical affliction.'

Veronica kept her eyes dead ahead and controlled her desire to look over her shoulder at the bar, and her handsome eligible boss and the blonde. Like a dog with a bone she asked, 'Is there one zygote in particular?'

'That's the thing. They last about as long as a bottle of milk, and then from nowhere a fresh milk bottle magically appears on his arm. Or in the fridge. Or however such an analogy should go.'

Well, what did you know? Mitch Hanover, for all the order-liness of his perfectly laundered button-down shirts, was a player. Could it be true that he wasn't on the lookout for someone to darn his socks and pour his nightcaps any more than she wanted to do those kinds of things? A dangerous little thrill scooted down Veronica's spine and landed in the backs of her knees.

She nodded. 'I get your drift.'

'Good. Now your turn. Do you find our boss yummy?'

Veronica waved a nonchalant hand in the air. 'Irrelevant.'

Kristin laughed. 'God, you're transparent. Just take my ad-vice and don't let the tall, dark and handsome man-about-town thing fool you, okay? There are more deep, gloomy chasms in that man's world than you or I would ever be likely to plumb in this lifetime.'

Before Veronica had the chance to find out more, Mitch's deep resonant voice echoed in her left ear. 'Good evening, ladies.'

She flinched so hard a glob of tomato pulp spilled out of her drink. She placed her glass carefully on the round table and looked up at Mitch with her most professional smile. 'Good evening, boss.'

He nodded her way, no hint of a smile, and she was sure that was all the acknowledgement she was going to get. Until his gaze lingered. For just a moment. But it was a moment in which she felt the sharp tang of electricity hit the back of her throat until she had to swallow in order to catch her breath. It was enough to make her wonder just what indulging in a little *fun* with the likes of straight-on-the-outside, mysterious-on-the-inside Mitch Hanover might be like.

Mitch finally blinked and turned his attentions to Kristin, and Veronica felt her whole body slump as though she'd been holding herself upright by nothing more than the strength of his piercing gaze.

'The gang have pushed a few tables together at the back of the bar,' he said, 'and ordered a round of some cocktail whose name I dare not repeat in polite company. Are you ready to join us?'

'You betcha,' Kristin said, pushing her chair back and toddling off in the direction of drinks paid for by someone else, leaving Veronica to deal with Mitch alone.

She rose more slowly, waiting until her loose black off-the-shoulder dress settled back around her knees before stepping out from behind the table.

Mitch stood politely by until she was up and walking before falling into step beside her. And while the bar was alive with the noise of happy-hour chatter, discreet music and the pleasant clink of ice on glass, a strange silence stretched taut between them.

Veronica took it upon herself to break it. 'So who's the blonde?'

Okay, so she had a big mouth. She couldn't help herself. Her mother had always claimed it was that quality that meant she could sell sea water to sailors. She worried it was that quality that made those same sailors read innocent flirtation as an invitation for so much more.

Mitch's expression barely changed. But it *did* change. She

saw a twitch in his cheek. It was the kind of twitch she was infamous for producing.

And just when she thought he was going to refrain from answering, he said, 'She's a friend.'

'Really? Where'd you find her? A campus social?'

The twitch morphed into a smile, which turned all too quickly into deep rumbling laughter that slithered sensually down Veronica's arms.

'I was wondering if I'd seen the most bumptious side of you in your interview,' he said.

'Heck, no. I was on my best behaviour.'

She thought that might be the end of the conversation until he glanced her way and explained, 'She works in the coffee shop at the bottom of my office building. As I left tonight she mentioned she'd heard we were going to be here so I asked her to join us.'

'Score one for Blondie,' she said. 'Though, do you think I hurt my apartment super's feelings when I didn't make the same offer after he asked where I was heading to tonight?'

At that he turned. The twitch twitched again, drawing the corner of his mouth into a truly intimate smile, one that came with a fierce twinkle in his eye.

She never should have willed the twinkle. It was far more potent than she possibly could have imagined. She had to scrunch her toes into her shoes to stop from tripping over her high, pointy size eights, which suddenly felt a size too small.

'Her name isn't Blondie, it's Stacy,' he said.

'Of course it is,' she muttered.

'With a y, no e, which for some reason she seems to think it important to remind me every few minutes.'

'Ha! Classic.'

He slowed so that she had no choice but to do the same or look as if she was running away from him. He blinked into her eyes for long enough she felt breathless all over, and she wished she hadn't opened her big mouth in the first place.

'Do you have a problem with my date?' he asked.

'Not at all,' she spluttered. 'It's not… It's just…'

'It's just?' he encouraged.

'She's just so…'

Young? Blonde? One-dimensional? Naff? Not good enough? Top-heavy?

In the end Veronica went with, 'She's just so very lovely.'

'Are you insinuating you didn't think I had it in me to pull someone so…very lovely?'

At his unexpectedly zesty choice of words Veronica barked out a laugh loud enough Kristin looked up from the table with far too smug an expression.

'No, not at all. I gather you're extremely…rich. And…and your vocabulary seems extensive. And you have a very nice array of suits. I'm sure there is all sorts of lovely out there just dying to be yours.'

Okay, so now she *really* wished she'd never opened her big mouth. The room suddenly felt very hot, especially in the region of her cheeks.

He came to a complete stop, a good three metres from the table where the Hanover House and Hanover Enterprises gangs, bar Boris who'd begged off as it was past his bedtime, were introducing themselves to one another.

Veronica again had no choice but to do the same. She turned to him, finding herself face to face. Close enough she could once again sense his signature aftershave. Could see the faint regrowth of his morning shave. Could decipher the million colours in his eyes, which ranged from smoky grey to shimmering quicksilver.

He held her eye contact as he told her, 'Stacy is in no way mine, Ms Bing.'

'Well, no, she's her own woman, I'm sure. As are we all.' She punched the air in a move that would have made Gloria Steinem proud.

A high-pitched giggle split the air and they both turned in the direction of the blonde, buxom, surely-below-the-age-of-twenty Stacy, with a *y* no *e*, who was in hysterics over something one of the drinks waiters had said. The waiter was concurrently mightily interested in her chest region, which didn't seem to bother her in the least.

'It was your vocabulary that put you over the line with that one, right?' Veronica asked, sarcasm dripping from her voice.

He leant sideways, dropped his voice to a wholly intimate rumble and said, 'I was quite sure it was the nice array of suits.'

And then he sauntered over to the table to take up position next to his date, leaving Veronica feeling unexpectedly out of her depth. Slightly baffled. And oddly exposed.

'So tell us about yourself, Veronica,' said Phil from Hanover Enterprises a good hour into the festivities. 'And not the stuff on your résumé. The juicy stuff. The stuff we can gossip about once we get back to work on Monday.'

Mitch leant back into his chair as he, like everyone else at the collection of tables, turned to the guest of honour.

As the first time he'd seen her, her dark, sun-tinted hair was wild and curled, though this time her lips were bare bar the lightest wash of gloss that caught the warmth of the trillion tiny down-lights scattered across the ceiling. She wore a string of see-through beads around her neck that didn't even pretend to be diamonds. And the lazy black dress draped over her curves with such relaxed informality looked as though it could simply fall off at any second.

He'd barely been able to keep his eyes dead ahead as he'd

walked next to her earlier just in case he was needed to come to the rescue with his jacket. At least that was what he told himself the reason had been.

She leant forward, elbows braced against the table, and grinned at every one of them, until her audience quieted, stilled and sat wholly in the palm of her hand. Though somehow her gaze had managed to glance off his nose as it had swept past him.

'Rightio. Things not on my résumé.'

Finally she looked his way, her eyes glowing with an intimate smile as she shared an in-joke just with him. It was enough to have him shifting on his seat.

'I'm five eight. Sagittarian. A little bit in love with the young Paul Newman, extremely in love with any kind of boot that stops just below the knee. My favourite colour is red and I do prefer gardenias and white gold if anybody's thinking of pooling together for a welcome gift of any kind. That the kind of thing you were after, Phil?'

Phil grinned, his slow-blinking eyes the sign of too much drink in his system already, as well as being completely besotted with the newcomer in his midst.

'Close,' he said. 'But I was hoping for some kind of sordid reason you had to move here. We can't fathom why you'd leave the sun and surf and beaches of the Gold Coast. So what was it? Jilted at the altar? Killed someone? Slept with the boss?'

As Mitch watched quietly on Veronica's happy façade slipped. The smile suffered, the light in her eyes dimmed, the brazen pose suddenly made her seem as if she were hiding behind her hands. The change in her was so subtle, the table so raucous, her visage still so bright and shiny he doubted anyone else even noticed the difference.

But he noticed, and he felt it as a wildly protective twinge in his gut.

Before he even knew what he was doing, he clapped his hands together so loudly the noise reverberated off the walls. But at least everyone looked his way as he called out, 'Right. Next round's on me. In fact, if you're quick off the mark I'll pick up the whole bar tab.'

The table cheered. Phil rocked back in his chair until it almost fell over. Orders poured in. Chairs scraped, the table jiggled and half the inhabitants left. And Veronica was forgotten. By everyone but him.

How could he forget her when her beautiful dark brown eyes looked back at him brimming with a mix of chagrin and thanks. In direct response his lungs tightened so hard, and so fast it felt as though they might be about to collapse in on themselves. And once again he was bemused that these reactions were actually happening to him.

His life since coming home to Melbourne had been lived with a kind of numbness. He wasn't silly enough not to know it had been a mostly self-induced haze, brought about by too much work, the bare minimum of time spent with his far too compassionate family, and what little social time he had left spent with women who did little to produce anything beyond a string of unmemorable nights.

But there was no denying it: the sass, the smarts, the way she could wind anyone around her little finger, Veronica Bing had his curiosity piqued to the point of discomfort.

Discomfort. That was the key word. Because there was nothing more to his attraction than desire and he knew there never could be. What he was feeling for her would only lead to an emotional dead end. Anything else he had to give had been left behind in London.

His current state was nothing a good long run and some brutal mental chewing out wouldn't burn away. In the meanwhile he'd keep his interests fluid, his hands off and his eyes roving to the Stacys of the world. Stacy was sweet. Unencumbered. And she was also trying to get his attention.

'Sorry?' he said, turning to face the warm and willing girl he'd practically ignored all evening while daydreaming about the one he ought to keep well away from.

Stacy stared up at him, more thought going on behind her pretty blue eyes than he'd imagined there could be. She looked from one eye to the other, smiled sadly, then said, 'Oh, never mind.'

She stood and headed into a quiet corner with the drinks waiter. Mitch considered heading over and staking his claim, but in the end he couldn't summon the energy to care. Instead his disobedient gaze swung to the brunette on the other side of the table, who as it turned out was watching him too.

'Not a drinker?' Veronica asked.

'Only when I'm thirsty. Is yours any good?'

She crossed her eyes and stared down into her thick red drink, then looked back up at him with a glimmer. 'It's doing the job.'

He picked himself up and moved around the table and took the seat next to hers. Her big brown eyes watched him all the way, and the closer he got, the more he saw that something Phil had said still stung. It was a concern. For him. As her employer. Period.

He looked off into the distance before asking, 'So why did you move down here from the Gold Coast? We never did cover that in our interview.'

'We didn't cover a lot of things. And think of how much time we saved.'

He glanced back her way. 'Lucky for us right now we have all the time in the world.'

She smiled but for the first time since he'd met her there was no humour behind it. And in the very same instant he realised that the change in her reeked of vulnerability, he felt an undeniable instability behind his ribs. He thumped a mental fist thereupon.

'I was born here,' she said.

'So Kristin told me. And?'

'And...I love nothing more than trying something new. Expanding my horizons. Kristin mentioned this job, it sounded perfect, so I came.'

'The Gold Coast job market saturated, is it?'

She opened her mouth, no doubt to make another smart comment, then snapped her lips tight together. In the end she went with, 'You're the one who looked so pained at offering me even a six-month contract. The fact that I'm not the kind of person looking to stick to one job, or one place, for the rest of my natural life should please you no end.'

His brow furrowed. 'So are you saying at the end of this six months you'll be gone?'

He looked from her right eye to her left, but for the first time since he'd met her she had managed to go into complete lockdown. The one time he really wanted to know what was going on behind those big brown eyes, her thoughts were her own.

'I'm no fortune-teller, so I have no idea what the future brings,' she said, 'but what I can promise is that while I'm here, I'm going to be the best thing that ever happened to you. In six months, well, perhaps you'll be ready to let me go, or perhaps I'll be ready to move on myself. Or maybe we'll still have some use for one another and I'll stay on. And I have the feeling that I'm not the only one here who's pretty happy with that arrangement.'

Smart, smart cookie. She's pinned you like a butterfly to a piece of foam, he thought. And right on top of that his brain went straight to, *And in six months she could well be gone*. He allowed himself to wonder just how significantly that changed the no-fly zone he'd built up around her.

Before his wondering brought about any solid conclusions Kristin came bounding up to the table. 'We're all heading to the Goo-Goo Bar,' she said. 'You guys in?'

Mitch raised an eyebrow. 'You're wondering if I might like to join you and the gang at a *nightclub*?'

She nodded, then stopped nodding and smiled sheepishly. 'Okay, so I said you'd laugh at me, but the others were hoping the bar tab might extend a little longer.'

'Tell the gang thanks, but no, thanks. To both the outing and the offer to pay their way.'

'Right. Veronica?' Kristin asked. 'You up for some boogy-ing on down?'

Mitch glanced at Veronica, who was stifling a yawn. She came out of it laughing. 'I think I might call it a night, as well.'

'You?' Kristin said, eyebrows disappearing somewhere deep into her hairline. 'The biggest party girl I've ever had the privilege to watch in action?'

'Says the girl who gave up her nose ring and dreadlocks for a beige suit and a twin set.'

Mitch's gaze spun to his assistant, who was blushing and glaring and mouthing who knew what to Veronica, who only grinned back.

'Either way,' Veronica said, 'Boris and I are meeting a carpenter at the gallery bright and early tomorrow.'

'A carpenter?' Mitch asked, dragging himself back to reality from the thought of Veronica dancing alone in the middle of a dimly lit dance floor with her eyes closed. 'On a Saturday?'

'Don't panic. We have superficial changes in mind. Truly. You'll hardly notice the difference.'

'Then why am I paying for it?'

'Because you told me you would.'

'Mmm.'

Kristin leant over and gave Veronica a kiss on the cheek. 'I'll talk to you tomorrow.' She then leant over as if to give Mitch a kiss too, suddenly remembered who he was, then reached out and shook his hand instead. Night, boss.'

'Goodnight, Kristin. See you Monday.'

She winked at Veronica, then skipped off to join the others.

Mitch uncurled himself and stood. Veronica grabbed her clutch purse from the table and did the same. Their eyes met and the smile she shot him was tired, tremulous and once again tinged with the tiniest hint of vulnerability. His solar plexus clenched, and his he-man instincts kicked into gear as though this woman had discovered the way to command them by remote control.

In an effort at self-preservation he looked dead ahead as he escorted her outside to the footpath, where she stopped. Assuming it was the dark keeping her at bay, he said, 'Allow me to walk you to your car.'

'No car. I caught a cab. Figured there'd be cocktails. And you'd be paying. Thought I'd make the most of it.' She grinned, wide and bright, but he knew she'd only had about a drink and a half all night.

'You go,' she said as though she'd sensed his hesitation. 'I'll be fine here. It's bright. People everywhere. A cab'll come along soon. This dress never fails.'

She grinned as if she was about to share some kind of in-joke, then, before his very eyes, she shook out her shoulders, dislodging the neckline of her dress which slithered sideways until his gaze became locked on the bare, tanned shoulder that had been exposed.

He swallowed hard, his eyes slowly moving up her neck, not at all sure he wanted to know what she was thinking by acting this way, but she wasn't paying him a lick of heed. Her back was to him as she looked up the street in search of a cab.

He looked to the dark heavens for support, but they just twinkled back at him benignly. And with the quiet of the night air giving him far too much space in his head, her words rang in his head. In six months she would be ready to move on. Until then she would be the best thing that had ever happened to him.

He snuck a glance sideways. Her dark curls were fluttering against her tanned cheek. Her bare shoulder lay within touching distance. She was temptation personified. Yet he was shrewd enough to know the built-in end-point to their affiliation made the idea of her even more appealing.

He ought to just go home. All he had to do was step past the gutter and he'd be on his way. But his feet stuck to the inside of his shoes like glue.

It was a mild night, though she hadn't brought any kind of wrap and he could tell, her having recently moved from the Tropics, she was shivering. She was stamping her feet against the pavement and the golden skin of her bare arms was tight with goose bumps.

When her teeth began to chatter, he knew he was done for. He glanced again at the starlit heavens. *Heaven help me*, he thought for the second time since meeting this woman.

He promised to add another two kilometres, uphill if at all possible, to the next morning's run as he said, 'Come on. I'll drive you home.'

CHAPTER THREE

VERONICA leant back against the headrest of Mitch's car. If her car was a reminder of the little girl with big dreams she had at one time been, Mitch's was the stuff of mid-life crises: luxurious, black, convertible. Though he didn't seem that close to mid-life. And further again from any kind of internal crisis. His skin was smooth, his shoulders broad and vitality oozed from his very pores.

The car purred to a comfortable stop on the rise of The Esplanade in St Kilda.

Veronica watched him from her pool of darkness in the passenger seat as his keen gaze skittered over the Luna Park fun park down the street and across the road at the imposing art deco magnificence of the Palais Theatre, beyond which the soft waves of St Kilda Beach lapped gently against a shallow stretch of sand.

'You really live here?' he asked.

Veronica leant forward and looked up at her apartment building. Within walking distance of more fabulous restaurants than a person had a right to know, it was exactly the kind of place she always lived: energetic, chic, cocooned by people galore so that she didn't feel as alone as she would otherwise.

She let go a lusty sigh. 'I'm happy to say I really do.'

'The noise will drive you mad,' he said.

And she found his words immensely comforting. Straight boss-man Mitch was back. Player Mitch had been left behind at the bar where he belonged. Meaning she had a good chance of getting to the front door without making a complete ninny of herself.

She shrugged. 'I've lived alone for a long time so I'm used to surrounding myself with white noise. I have the stereo on 24/7 as it is, so a bit of laughter and merriment spilling through my windows certainly won't get in my way.'

He leant over the steering wheel, his brow furrowing as he took in the ageing façade of her building with its flaky cream paint and bars on the windows.

Veronica laughed, the tension that had settled over her shoulders from the moment he'd chosen to sit with her rather than follow his date finally dissipating. 'It's okay, Mitch. It's secure. It's solid. And I'm a big girl. Have been for some years. I can take care of myself.'

He leant back into the plush lambswool-covered seat and actually looked at her for the first time since she'd hopped in his car. 'You can, can you?' he asked.

She lifted her chin. 'You bet your bottom dollar.'

He nodded slowly, over and over again, as though she'd given him the right answer. And by the sudden gleam in his eyes she wasn't altogether sure she wanted to know what the question had been.

She hurried up and said, 'Therefore I can take it from here.'

'Nevertheless,' he said, before hopping out of the car.

Too late to stop him, she gathered her purse, fixed her skirt and reached out for the door handle only to find her door had been opened for her.

She looked up in surprise to find Mitch standing before her.

He was backlit by the streetlamps above. All dark hair, dark suit and dark eyes. And old-fashioned gentlemanly manners. Her heart gave a sudden, treacherous thumpety thump in her chest.

'I haven't had a man open a car door for me since my dad,' she blurted.

'I'm sorry to hear that.'

'Not as sorry as I am to say it.' Her eyelashes fluttered against her cheeks as she looked down at the cracked concrete and alighted from the car, knees together as her equally old-fashioned mum had taught her.

'Thank you,' she said, her voice low and husky.

'My pleasure.'

He leant across and closed the car door behind her. She was soon enclosed in a cloud of his scent. It was clean, crisp, expensive. And so very him. A glutton for punishment, she breathed in through her nose and closed her eyes.

When she opened them again she realised just how close they stood. Suddenly not knowing what to do with her hands, Veronica rubbed them down her arms. The night was mild enough, but still her skin felt kind of tingly. And the world around them strangely quiet. Too quiet.

'Don't you think my apartment building looks rather pretty in the moonlight?' she said.

He paused, for the briefest moment, then said. 'It certainly does.'

Though she couldn't see his eyes, she knew they'd never once left her. And the reason behind her tingly skin became clear. Mitch Hanover, her cool-as-a-cucumber boss, a man with far more gentlemanly tendencies than a girl with her lifestyle had been used to, was thinking things he ought not to be thinking. Which in turn made her decision to not think things she ought not to be thinking downright redundant.

She glanced back at him. The moon had come out from behind a cloud and a silver beam slanted across his deep grey eyes. They were not watching her the way they'd watched her during their interview. The bemusement was still there, but now it was only in place as a cover to conceal a wave of something far stronger. Something that looked a heck of a lot like desire.

Veronica's heart no longer thumped. It tumbled. In the quiet evening street, without noise, or hustle and bustle or the insulation of other people, she felt the same desire. Like sparks shooting between them as physically as if she'd run her socked feet along a stretch of carpet.

It felt as though the next one of them to move, to blink, to speak, would decide which course their tenuous relationship would follow.

Mitch finally looked at his watch, frowned and said, 'Come on, I'll walk you to your door and then I really must get going.' And when he looked back at her, the bemusement was firmly back in place.

Just like that the spell had been broken.

That was a close one, she thought, shaking off the knowledge that she had all too easily opened herself to the possibility of the man when the truth was he was the ultimate impossibility. Bad, bad Veronica.

'Poor Mitch,' she said. 'If we'd known seven o'clock drinks would take so much out of a man of your years, we could have moved the date to a Sunday matinee.'

Without waiting to see how he took her words, she turned and headed towards the high brick wall separating the apartment block from the footpath.

'I've never known a woman who so delighted in provoking a man, Ms Bing,' he said from close behind her.

'Provoking, Mr Hanover?' She pressed in her PIN number to open the squeaky black wrought iron gate, then turned to him with a flat smile, thankful the semi-darkness hid the still feverish warmth of her cheeks. 'I'm engaging in a civil conversation with my boss, that's all.'

He leant his shoulder against the concrete wall and slid his hands into his pockets. If she'd had a camera on her she could have made a quick buck shooting him for *GQ* no problem. 'If this is what you call civil,' he said, 'I do fear for those less able to cope with civil than I.'

'Fear not. Those less able tend to get swept to the wayside before they are even aware I've been and gone.'

His eyes were dark. Still. Dark and unfairly delicious. She tried to break eye contact. She really did. But he was far, far too worthy of being looked at.

'Did you leave someone less able behind on the Gold Coast?' he asked, his voice deep and persuasive.

'Well, so much for being civil,' she muttered as she pushed through the gate and kept walking.

Mitch followed her down the curving path. The full moon shone silver light through the gaps in the ivy covered trellis winding above. It would have been terribly romantic if only he weren't him and she weren't her.

Apparently not getting the hint that she didn't want to talk about it, Mitch continued, 'I only ask because as your boss I want you to know that I expect you to see out your contract. You wanted six months, I gave it. Therefore for the totality of that time you belong to me.'

'I thought you said no woman belonged to you.'

He took a breath. 'By *me*, I meant Hanover Enterprises.'

'Well, that's fine, so long as Hanover Enterprises realises it's sharing me for the next six months with the landlord of this place whose contract was scarier than yours, and with the bank who truly owns my car. It appears that I belong to nobody, least of all myself.'

'I'm glad to hear it,' Mitch said, his voice dropping to a rumble in the eerie quiet. And again she felt as though she was helping the guy tick off a list, though she had no real idea of what the list was about.

'You wouldn't be the first,' she said, keeping her eyes dead ahead as she reached into her purse for her keys. 'My door's all the way around the back. I really can take it from here.'

'We've come this far,' he said, 'why stop now?'

'Right,' she said, letting the word stretch out before letting go a grandiose sigh and leading him through the concrete archway, past the old fountain with its pair of mossy cherubs that looked as if it hadn't been turned on in a good decade and to the back cobbled path of her apartment building.

If the front road had seemed quiet, this place was worse. She could hear the sounds of his breathing, slow and deep. The click clack of her footsteps on the uneven ground. And worse, the voices in her head that sounded a distant warning that with every step towards her front door Mitch Hanover was entering the realm of *the current man in her life*.

Even if nothing happened between them, even if the strange and sudden compulsion she felt towards him never eventuated into anything beyond 'provocation', even though they were not destined to work in one another's pockets as she and Geoffrey had, even though he seemed as able to take care of himself as she was, even though Mitch had never once looked at her with white picket fences in his eyes, it would pay to be super cautious.

Why, oh, why did life have to be so complicated?

When they reached her ground-floor apartment, she turned to face him, lips thinned, chin firm, sensibilities firmly back in place. She again rubbed her hands down her arms. 'I'd forgotten how chilly it gets here at night.'

'It's over twenty degrees,' he said, the sound skittering through the darkness to send her sensitive skin into some kind of overdrive of sensation.

'As I said…' She added a hearty, 'Brrrrr,' in the hopes of leavening the tension. It worked. Sort of.

Mitch laughed. His was such a nice laugh, husky, deep, rumbling, and it took all sorts of parts of him in order to make it work. His mouth, his cheeks and mostly his eyes. It lit them with a glimmer that did things to her midriff that the unplumbed depths of those same eyes had earlier done to her heart.

She mentally slapped herself and decided then and there she'd simply not look him in the eyes anymore. For the next five months and three weeks. Then she'd be just fine.

'Thanks for the drink, boss, and the lift and the escort.' She jingled her keys and stepped as far away from him as she could without looking as if that was what she was trying to do.

'My pleasure, Ms Bing,' he said, with a gallant nod that reminded her of him opening her car door. And the door at the bar. And pulling out her chair when she'd been interviewed. He was not only beautiful, and driven and together, he was an honest-to-goodness gentleman. A rarer bird than she had even supposed. Her thumpety thumping heart instead began to pitter-patter and she knew the time had come to call the evening quits.

'Well, goodnight!' she sing-songed, finally finding her very best killer grin and using it for all she was worth. 'Don't let the bedbugs bite.'

Mitch watched her again for a few long moments. Her badly behaved skin began to hum. And when she realised he was leaning in to kiss her on the cheek it vibrated until it burned.

And then something, later she couldn't for the life of her think what she could have done to encourage it, but something made him change his mind. At the very last second Mitch changed tack and pressed his lips to hers.

Light as a feather. With as little pressure as if he were kissing her hand. But his kiss felt anything but innocent.

It felt like magic. Like fairy dust. As if the planets had aligned to shoot beams of heaven through the moonlight. And for a girl like Veronica, who'd once upon a time sat alone and lonely in her suburban bedroom dreaming of such things, though had not seen all that much in the way of effortless magic and moonlight in her twenty-six years, it was a revelation.

Ignoring her conscience, every ounce of sense and the protective rules she was determined to live by, even though she couldn't for the life of her remember in that moment what they were, she closed her eyes and kissed him right on back.

If Mitch hadn't meant anything by it, that was the moment for him to pull away. She waited for it, held her breath, even imagining the decrease in pressure and trying to come up with a funny platitude to excuse her actions.

But then, oh, so gently he tilted, opened his mouth and deepened the kiss. It remained slow, subtle, sweet, unexpected. And hotter than the Gold Coast sun at the height of summer.

Her shoulders slumped as she melted towards him. Her fingers went lax and her brain turned to mush. His tongue eased out and ran lightly over her top teeth and such swirls of bright light flashed behind her closed eyes she wasn't sure how she managed to stay upright.

And then, all too soon, he pulled away as easily as he had come to her.

Veronica's eyes fluttered back open. Mitch's deep grey eyes

remained in darkness. There was no way she could tell what he was thinking. No way to find the right note with which to say goodnight. To know if this was the beginning of something she didn't want or the end of something she suddenly wanted so badly her heart actually ached.

Oh, rats! What had she gone and done?

Mitch saved her from standing there, mute and panicked for the rest of time. His voice was consolingly rough as he said, 'I think it's past time I left you to your evening.'

'No argument here,' she managed to get out through her thick throat.

'Goodnight, Veronica.'

And he had to go and use her name like that, didn't he? Rather than the offhanded Ms Bing. As if a shift in their arm's-length relationship had truly occurred.

'Goodnight, boss,' she threw back, hoping it might create some semblance of a bridge back to the much more simple enmity they'd had merely hours before.

'Sweet dreams,' he said, and then he turned and left. And she watched him the whole way, his broad form a chasm of darkness shifting through the moonlit, overgrown path.

She turned towards her door and let her forehead thump against it with a satisfying thud. She tried convincing herself Mitch had no idea her dreams would be all about what had just happened, but it was a waste of time.

Mitch Hanover was a smart guy. And, as evidenced by what he'd done to her with that one small kiss, he was also an experienced guy. His skill level was so incredibly high he could have gone pro.

He knew how to kiss, he knew what her dreams would be about before she'd ever dreamt them, and he now knew that she wasn't smart enough not to get involved with her boss.

While she questioned how she could be three thousand kilometres away yet right back where she'd started.

The following days of chilly spring rain were another shock to
Veronica's system, which was far more used to tropical days
and balmy nights.

But for the glossy, glamorous, whiz-bang opening night pre-
show of Hanover House's quarterly Big Australian Art and
Antique Auction the heavens put on a glisteningly clear, starry
starry night.

The good weather didn't turn out to be enough to stop
Veronica from asking herself, 'What the hell am I doing here?'
at least once every two minutes.

She ran sweaty palms down her new tight red tartan pencil
skirt, lifted her leg and ran a shaky finger inside the heel of one
of her lucky three-inch-high red stiletto mules to make sure it
was sitting comfortably, took a deep breath, then slid slowly
and silently through the thankfully large crowd.

She listened in on conversations and paid attention to
language people were using to describe certain pieces, as she
had every intention of using those exact words to her advantage on the day of the auction itself. But as to winding her way
into an actual conversation? So far, her luck had been thin on
the ground, hence the rising panic.

It hadn't taken long for her to realise that this was no comic-
book convention or used-car auction. These people were like
something out of an old Katharine Hepburn movie. Elegant,
haughty, imperious. She'd managed to befriend one or two at
most. And any others who'd actually looked her in the eye
didn't even try to hide the fact they thought she was way below
them in the food chain.

And for the first time since she'd arrived back in Melbourne the seeds of self-doubt took root. The years she'd spent looking after her mum while those of her generation earned degrees and got their feet wet in the workplace felt as if they were again catching up with her faster than she could outrun them.

After a good twenty minutes of feeling as if she wasn't making much headway, she'd built up a fairly impressive head of steam that the one person who ought to have been there to give her support on this big night wasn't.

She hadn't spent all evening watching the front door for Mitch's arrival. A good portion of it, sure, but certainly not all. Though the times she had she'd taken solace in imagining slapping him upside the back of the head for a) not calling her after the other night, b) getting Kristin to return any business calls she'd made to his office during the five-odd days since and c) becoming such a regular feature in her dreams she'd taken to sleeping in fits and starts, which hadn't made her preparation for this night any easier.

She needn't have bothered fretting. The moment he arrived the energy in the room changed. The steady hum of upper-class voices lifted a notch as if they knew their prince had come. And the telltale hairs on the back of her neck stood on end.

She turned to the door and saw him. And her breath was sapped from her lungs. Even surrounded by a plethora of social elite decked out in their best designer casuals, he was just that much taller, that much darker, that much more the matinee idol with every inch of him sewn and stitched together as if to some kind of perfect God-given pattern. The hopeless cad.

'Veronica Bing,' a weak male voice said. She turned, aggravated from sending daggers to an unaware Mitch, to find a five-foot-nothing man in a badly fitted tweed suit smiling up at her. 'My name is Charles Grosse. I'm an agent and will be bidding on the auction for a number of private collectors. You may have heard of me?'

Veronica bit her lip. Great! Why couldn't Charles have sought her out half an hour before when she was feeling like a Nigel No Friends? Because now, head of steam or not, she needed to talk to Mitch, needed some of his cool to rub off on her before she fair exploded from nervous tension.

'Lovely to meet you, Charles,' she said, holding out her hand for a quick shake. 'There's plenty here to catch the eye of a discerning man such as yourself.'

She shifted so that Charles stood between her and Mitch, as thankfully the man was short enough she could see over his head.

'Oh, there's one or two things that have taken my fancy,' he said.

She blinked and looked down at the man who now had her hand in both of his, massaging her palm with his slightly damp fingers. Oh, heck! Now *this*? Really?

'Well, Charles, I promise you once you've had a load of our *hors d'oeuvre* table, especially the crab puffs, you'll be smitten.'

She slowly extricated herself from his grip and lay a hand on his back to give him the slightest shove towards the back of the room where crab puffs and more awaited, then she slid through a gap in the crowd as fast as she could, her eyes searching out her boss.

He moved through the crowd, shaking hands, kissing cheeks, smiling easily and nodding as the gathered masses engulfed him as one of their own. She looked in his wake for a zygote blonde but couldn't find one. It might not have meant anything, but it foolishly gave her a much-needed kick in the confidence stakes.

'Their bark is far worse than their bite,' a smoky-voiced woman said from behind her.

Veronica turned away from staring at Mitch to find a lean, lanky, fiftysomething woman dressed in a powder-blue trouser suit with delicate pearls strung about her neck and ears.

'I'm sorry?'

The woman waved a long-fingered hand at the room in general. 'Nights like this are all about scoping out the competition. The people in this room have known one another for generations. They know exactly what one another can spend on the goodies hereabouts. A stranger in their midst might well add an extra zero to any purchase made. Don't take the sideways looks personally.'

Veronica's shoulders slumped. 'Am I that obvious?'

The woman laughed. 'Only to a discerning eye. So have you picked a favourite?'

'Client or auction item?'

The woman's gaze slid to hers and stayed, and for a moment Veronica felt as though her pale blue eyes could see into the bottom of her soul.

'Oh, I like you,' the woman said.

Veronica laughed, the feeling loosening all her stiff bits beautifully. 'Spread the word, please. Now, you go first. Which is your favourite piece?'

'Follow me.'

Veronica respectfully let the woman lead the way through the growing crowd, passing carved wooden furnishings, walls covered in small framed paintings and glass cases filled with objects both sparkly and dull, old and very old, all Australian made, until they hit a far corner of the room.

'Here,' the woman said.

Veronica looked over her shoulder to find a tray of medals and jewellery lying snug atop a slightly frayed navy velvet pillow that she'd insisted the gallery gang fray further to give it a shabby-chic look rather than an I've-been-encased-in-out-of-date-mothballs-for-the-past-five-years look.

Among the highlighted pieces, and at the end of the woman's pointed finger, was a ring: a thin white gold band encrusted with tiny diamond fragments and set with a glittering princess cut diamond. The solitaire was relatively small, the band no longer perfectly round, but Veronica couldn't take her eyes off it. It looked…sad, and lonely, as if its purpose in life had been ful-filled a long time ago and now it didn't know what it was meant to be.

Her heart gave a little shudder before she coughed it back into place. Feeling empathy for an old ring was nuts. Beyond nuts; it was schmaltzy. Yet she had to clear her throat before asking, 'Has it some kind of historical significance?'

'It was my husband's grandmother's ring,' the woman said.

'Your…? Oh, how lovely. But why sell it?'

She knew the moment the words were out of her mouth it was incredibly tactless. The woman could be standing there in her last designer original while living on nothing but old tinned apples at home. Maybe the ring reminded her of her own lost love. Or maybe she was a chronic gambler and needed the quick buck. Veronica had seen guys sell baseball cards, classic cars and houses for lesser reasons again and again.

The woman said, 'Selling a piece of our family history at every auction held here has been our trademark since the business began. It proves we stand behind our name.'

Veronica suddenly felt lost, as if she was a chapter behind in the conversation.

'I'm Miriam Hanover,' the woman explained.

And the light finally dawned. This gem of a woman was Mitch's mother. She should have recognised the measured in-telligence in her eyes and instant appeal right away.

'Veronica Bing,' she said, and held out a hand which Miriam shook before turning back to the ring with a slightly wistful expression on her face.

'I had hoped my Mitch might one day find some use for it, but since the events in London his interests have been determinedly set upon bright, shiny, *expendable* things. Especially those with dyed blonde hair.'

If the lady's name hadn't left Veronica halfway to speechless, that sure did. Especially when her gaze shifted north to Veronica's own dark waves and back again to her eyes.

She couldn't know that Mitch's attention had recently veered off said course. She couldn't! But then again what was there to know? Nothing, that was what. A moonlight kiss and then nothing. She hoped her eyes managed to get that across. Not the kiss part, just the nothing part.

'And fast cars,' Miriam said, letting her off the hook with aplomb. 'But though the former is a relatively new development, one we all hope he will grow out of in good time, the latter I fear is quite simply a boy thing. My husband has always been the same way. Show him a car with racing stripes and he'll dribble on his shoes.'

Veronica smiled as she realised she was meant to do, even though she still felt as though she was missing something. As if everyone thought she was in on the joke about Mitch, but she'd arrived ten minutes too late.

'Mother, leave the poor woman alone,' Mitch's smooth-as-silk voice said from somewhere far too near her right ear.

Then he leant between them to kiss his mother on the cheek and Veronica swallowed and kept her gaze dead ahead.

It was the first time she'd seen Mitch up close and personal since the kiss. She'd decided after the third day without contact that it had, in fact, meant nothing as Melbournians were obviously more touchy feely than she remembered them being. But now, here, beside him, his scent wafting past her nose, his large form encroaching on her personal space until she found herself swaying towards him, it felt like anything but nothing.

Thankfully Miriam's voice cut through her shambolic intro-spection before she could do anything so ill-advised as grab-bing a handful of his jacket and dragging him to some quiet corner of the room where she could beg him to tell her what kind of stunt he was trying to pull.

'I was just telling Veronica here a little of the background of Nanna's ring so that she can use it in her spiel next week.'

Mitch's brow came together in a series of horizontal lines before he understood what she was saying. His gaze zeroed in on the ring, which still sat quietly nestled on its navy vel-vet cushion.

'That's what you've chosen to auction?'

Miriam nodded. 'It has been sitting in my dresser gathering dust all these years. I thought perhaps the time had come to let it go. Unless of course you'd prefer we hang on to it.'

He continued to stare at the small ring. Enough that Veronica looked back at it, as well, biting back the growing desire to throw her hands in the air and yell, *Will somebody please tell me what I'm missing?*

She glanced up at Mitch who blinked, and blinked again, before his face cleared and he looked back to his mother with all the ap-pearance of a man without a care in the world. 'Sell it. Now, the Jenkinsons were asking after you. Time to schmooze.'

'Fine.' Miriam gave her son a kiss on the cheek, then pointed a long manicured finger Veronica's way. 'And you, my sweet girl, are coming back home with us for supper tonight once the show's over.'

Veronica looked to Mitch, her mouth agape, sure he would

fill her silence with a convincing excuse why that wouldn't be proper. Mitch who hadn't actually looked her in the eye since arriving. Hot-and-cold Mitch who had, more than once, regarded her as if she was something precious, and then in the blink of a pair of flat grey eyes appeared to see her as the thorn in his side. Mitch whose face was now a mask of impassiveness.

It was enough for her contrary nature to rear its ugly head.

'Miriam,' she said, 'I can't think of a nicer offer I've had since coming to town. I'd be delighted to come for supper.'

Mitch's cheek twitched and Veronica felt a small victory.

'Lovely. Now, I must see to the Jenkinsons. Gorgeous couple. And two of our biggest spenders,' she added with a wink. 'Mitch can give you directions, all right?'

Miriam left in a wave of Chanel, and Mitch and Veronica were alone again. Thankfully this time amidst a crowd of people.

When Mitch didn't look as if he was going to strike up a conversation anytime soon, or leave her to her own devices, Veronica gave in and asked, 'So, what do you think?'

'About what?'

She clenched her fists to stop herself from thumping him on the arm for being so damned impervious. Or perhaps she ought to be thumping herself for not being impervious enough. What a pair.

'Oh, I don't know,' she said. 'The dozen-odd cosmetic changes we've spent the past two weeks busting a gut to implement before this huge night in the hopes of saving your skin.'

Mitch's gaze sharpened on goodness knew what in the distance. 'My skin is just fine.'

She finally gave in and threw her hands in the air. The guy was just so…ggggrrrrrrr!!! 'Fine. Have a nice night, Mitch. Try the crab puffs. They're heavenly.'

She made to move away, when a hand clamped down on her upper arm. Long, warm fingers burned into her bare skin creating a wave of sensation that shimmied through her body until it pooled in her empty stomach.

She turned and glared at her boss, doing her best to decipher what was happening behind those impermeable grey depths. And what she saw, of all things, was contrition. His eyes were soft and endearing, his mouth curved into a sexy self-deprecating smile. If she'd ever wondered how he managed to score himself a blonde a minute, she had no reason to wonder anymore.

And then he had to go and say, 'Forgive me,' and she fair melted beneath his touch.

Especially when her mind tumbled with ideas about all the things he could be apologising for. The kiss? Not talking to her since the kiss? Not throwing her over his shoulder and carting her inside her apartment and ravishing her senseless after the kiss? Or had his apology nothing whatsoever to do with the kiss, which his mother had intimated might be as daily an occurrence for him as driving a flashy fast car?

She slowly twisted her arm out of his grip and he just as slowly let her go. She shook her hair off her warm neck and looked him dead in the eye as she said, 'Tell me the place looks fantastic and I'll think about forgiving you.'

His sexy smile kicked up a notch, as did her heart rate. 'First tell me what it cost me and then I'll tell you if I like it.'

Right. The kiss *had* been irrelevant. A momentary lapse of reason. A temporary glitch in the boss-employee relationship. Tonight, he was back to being all business, which was just how she preferred things to remain.

She crossed her arms across her chest in order to quell the obstinate surge of disappointment clutching at her. 'What if I told you the refurb cost half what I asked for in the interview?'

'Did you say half?' His eyebrows slid as high as they could go and she finally felt his attention was fully on her. Mitch Hanover *was* all business. She was beginning to understand why the blondes didn't last long.

'Okay, two thirds,' she admitted, 'but still I think myself fairly brilliant.'

And then, just to throw her off balance, as though they were having a regular conversation between a man and a woman who just happened to have kissed at one time, he laughed his deep, rumbling laugh and she bit the inside of her lip to stop from sighing at the gorgeous sound.

'So long as you remember I didn't hire you to decorate the place—I hired you to sell lots of artefacts for more than their asking price. To prove to those who've put their faith in us to sell their family heirlooms that we are worth the risk. And to show those who fork out their hard-earned dosh that we are still well and truly here. Do that and then I'll think about admitting you're brilliant,' he said, and all with the kind of leisurely smile that had put Cary Grant on the map.

Veronica wanted to hit him. She really did. She'd never met anyone who could be so charming and so infuriating all at once.

She looked away, out over the crowd, and caught the eye of Charles Grosse, who wiggled his fingers at her. She let her gaze glance off the top of his head as she asked, her voice as sharp as vinegar, 'No Stacy tonight?'

Without preamble Mitch's voice dropped. He turned his back on the crowd and leant in to murmur against her ear the words, 'Not tonight.'

And, rather than feeling as if she'd scored a point, she felt exactly as she had standing outside her apartment building, certain to the centre of her very bones that business was suddenly the last thing he was thinking about. If she wasn't careful, this guy could well send her scurrying to the Funny Farm for the Emotionally Unhinged.

A madly waving hand from the other side of the room flickered in the corner of her vision. If it was Charles Grosse and his damp hands, she'd decided he was the lesser of two evils. Thankfully it was the lovely Boris. She was so relieved she could have kissed him.

'I'd better go,' she said. 'Duty calls.'

She moved as fast as her high red heels would carry her, thankful to their soles that this time Mitch didn't move to stop her.

CHAPTER FOUR

MITCH leant against a wall draped in lavish hot pink velvet.

That's new, he thought. As was the sumptuous, highly contemporary dark chocolate lounge suite in the middle of the room, which clashed quite magnificently with the aged antiquities to be found scattered in glass cases and on the newly painted shiny white walls around the room.

The place did indeed look so different he'd paused halfway up the stairs and leant back looking for the Hanover House signage when he'd first arrived. It was bright, vibrant, on the verge of being gauche, yet somehow not. If he had to find one word for the new ambience that word would have been *vital*.

The patrons were spending almost as much time touching the tactile furnishings and commenting on the abundance of mismatched chandeliers glittering from the ceiling as they were looking at the wares. The businessman in him would rather they'd spent more time perusing the art than the renovation, but all of the clients were smiling and drinking the free champagne, and talking about Hanover House in such a way as he hadn't heard in…well, ever.

He felt the winds of change ruffling the hairs on the back of his neck. Whether those winds would be fair or ill, he would find out soon enough.

A microphone crackled. Someone cleared their throat noisily, and as one the inhabitants of the room turned towards the small stage at the back of the gallery.

There, behind a perfectly professional conservative, stained-oak podium stood Veronica Bing. Dark waves cascading over her bare shoulders, frou-frou black frills spilling down the front of her sleeveless shirt, and below the waist curves squeezed magnificently into a red tartan skirt that stopped just below her knees, giving her a modicum of good taste all the while making her the most glaringly sexy woman in the room.

The fact that having kissed her he now knew how she tasted, how soft her skin truly was and how delicately scented her hair, didn't hurt that opinion one little bit.

'Is this thing on?' Veronica said, tapping at the microphone.

Mitch clenched all over as the room twittered.

'I guess that's a yes,' Veronica said, a self-deprecating smile sliding across her face. 'Anyhow, for those of you who haven't been accosted by me as yet, my name is Veronica Bing and I'm delighted to let you all know that I am the new in-house auctioneer for Hanover House. To squash the rumours before they take root, yes, I came from the Gold Coast, but don't hold that against me. Beneath this tan I am a born and bred Melbourne girl. So, Bernie Walden, where are you?'

Like good little acolytes, the crowd turned to the centre of the room where Bernie, sporting-goods manufacturer, football-club president, true art connoisseur and by far the richest man in the room, blushed beetroot-red.

'Bernie, I'm taking that bet. Your Cats to my Magpies at this weekend's footy, okay?'

Bernie shot her a salute, then did his best to disappear into the floor.

She leant onto the podium then, looking as though she was

about to bestow a great secret. Her backside scooted backwards, her right leg bent behind her showing off a killer red shoe at the end of her shapely calf. If she hadn't had every man in the room at her disposal as yet, she did now.

'I feel an energy in the room tonight, my friends, and it tells me that next Friday's Hanover House Big Australian Art and Antique Auction is going to be the most exciting event this room, this *town* has ever seen. So bring your wallets, and prepare to lose your shirts, and more importantly your hearts, to the stunning array of beautiful must-haves right now hovering dazzlingly just out of your reach. Until then, drink up, schmooze, peruse and imagine just how that brooch, or that chair, or that painting would fit beautifully in your home. Because come next Saturday, they could all be yours. So long as the person standing next to you right now doesn't get there first.'

She bowed away from the mike and rapturous applause broke out and spread through the room. The crowd was mesmerised. And it hadn't taken a spotlight, a sale sign or intrigue in watching a venerated house of business crash and burn to do it. It had taken a curvaceous, vivacious, brunette power pack.

Standing up there on the dais, she was a bright, shiny livewire of a creature. Skin so warm and brown she looked as if she'd seen more sunshine in the past three months than he had in years. With a raucousness in her smile, an untameable bearing in her dark curls and crinkles around her eyes that proved she wasn't afraid to smile, or wrinkle or care.

In fact, she carried such bravado around her like a cloak he wondered if she was afraid of anything.

He'd known a woman with that fearless streak only once before now. And being with her had given him the most joy and the most pain he'd ever known. Enough of both to last a lifetime. Enough that by the time he'd moved back to

Melbourne without her he'd gone about systematically shutting off every kind of passion rattling around in the cavernous places inside him, lest he find himself in a position to feel that depth of emotion again.

He watched Veronica Bing shake hands with everyone as she made her way down the stairs and through the crowd. He could only imagine how sore her hand would be the next day.

She might have been fearless, but she was otherwise so very different from studious, focussed, delicate Claire with her soft auburn hair, her twin sets and tweed trousers, smiling up at him over her dainty glasses as she worked on her dissertation over the kitchen table, they could have been different species.

'You've picked a winner there,' a familiar husky voice said from behind him.

Mitch blinked and turned to find his mother. For a moment he thought she was talking about Claire. Claire whose image he normally kept locked away behind a steel trap, and who had made more personal appearances in his mind in the past week than she had in the past year.

But he quickly realised his mother was watching Veronica with a wide smile on her face. Veronica, who was taking up more space inside his head than any woman had since Claire.

Confused, bemused, unimpressed with himself, he turned away and focussed on an unfixed point in the distance. 'I can't claim all the credit. She's Kristin's friend from university.'

'Don't be modest. I'm proud you were able to see past the end of your own nose to recognise that shoving her out the door would be the silliest decision you'd ever made.'

'I'm hardly that callous.'

'Callous? No, of course you're not. Tunnel-visioned, perhaps. Or at least that's what I was beginning to fear. Until now. Yes, she is exactly the breath of fresh air we all need around here.'

'She's only on a six-month contract, Mother. I warn you now not to get too attached.'

'Six months' worth of genuine attachment is far better than six lifetimes with none, as you well know.' She squeezed his arm and kissed his cheek. 'See you at home soon, darling. And I'm counting on you to make sure our little friend gets there nice and safe.'

Nice and safe, Mitch thought, wondering what his mother was worried about. Veronica had enough chutzpah he had the feeling she could take better care of herself in a dark alley than he could.

As though she sensed him watching her, Veronica glanced his way, only half an ear listening to the encroaching Armadale crowd, no doubt lathering her with praise and advice, which she ought to have been lapping up.

But once their eyes locked they stayed locked.

She was a good ten metres away, across the other side of a room teeming with people, yet still, it took nothing more than the stroke of that alluring gaze to make his skin warm, his back straighten, his thoughts turn to imagining what might happen if he bellowed, 'Alien invasion!' and the room cleared, leaving just the two of them and that comfortable-looking couch.

Her brows snuck together in question. Yet her smile only grew, her dark red lips lifting just for him. His warm skin soon began to burn in anticipation.

And he remembered in a flash of pain and anger why it had been a blessing that he hadn't had this kind of a smouldering physical reaction to a woman in a long while. It only served to remind him in Technicolor detail the last time he'd felt anything along the same lines, and how torturous it had been to have those feelings torn away.

He gave Veronica a chummy thumbs-up. Her brow

smoothed and she nodded in acceptance of his flimsy praise. Then he turned away and headed for the bar for a much-needed finger of Scotch.

He vowed then that Veronica Bing would no longer need protection from the likes of him.

As to the kind of protection he might need from her? That was his cross to bear.

As the crowd around her dispersed Veronica watched Mitch walk away, her racing heart clogging her throat.

She knew the sensation was partly due to her recent public speech, but it had, if anything, only become worse when she'd caught him watching her so seriously from the other side of the room.

For what she'd seen in his eyes had shifted everything inside her until she could no longer catch her breath with quite the same ease as she'd always been able to up until that point in her life.

Mitch had given her a thumbs-up. He'd smiled. To all intents and purposes he'd seemed his regular aloof self. But she'd seen something in his eyes that had floored her.

An unexplained ache had emanated from him in waves until she'd felt it fair across the room. She'd recognised it. The raw, enveloping sadness. She'd been there herself on nights when all the music or white noise, or company in the world couldn't blanket the memory of losing those she loved most in the world.

Why *he* might so ache, she had no idea. He had it all. Beauty, brains, money, charm, a loving family all intact and perfect. But there was no denying what she'd seen. What she'd *felt*.

If liking him and kissing him had her confused, this impression made her feet feel as if they'd been swept out from under her. And her heart fractured. She felt the cracks appear and broaden with each beat. A trickle of her natural empathy slipped through, spreading through her body like a current. And caring to that kind of degree was exactly what she'd spent the past few years of her life so vigilantly trying to avoid.

'You were fantastic!' Kristin screamed in Veronica's ear before enveloping her in a bear hug.

Veronica jumped so hard she stubbed her toe in the point of her right shoe. She hopped on one foot until the pain passed. 'I didn't make a complete dunce of myself?'

'Nah. They loved you. They're so used to people like us bowing every time they pass, you were like the coolest thing they'd seen in an age. You practically dared them to leave without buying anything. Fabulous!'

Veronica grabbed a flute of pink champagne from a passing waiter, more to give her still-trembling hands something to do than anything else.

'Mitch gave me a thumbs-up, then he disappeared,' she said, hoping to get some kind of inside information from Kristin without seeming too obvious. 'You don't think he's on the phone to his lawyer right now looking for a way to fire me?'

Kristin scoffed. 'Don't worry about Mitch. So long as there's a turnout and a profit, he'll be happy. Well, maybe not happy, I don't know that I've ever seen the guy happy the way normal people are happy, but he'll be satisfied. Though come to think of it the boss man hasn't been able to find a thing to grumble about tonight. It's a miracle. In fact, he's been so smiley and cordial I'd go as far as saying this past week he's been a changed man, if it wasn't for the fact that I know how deceptively smooth he can be when he wants to be. I can't for the life of me imagine what's going on inside that steel trap of a head of his, though I'd love to know so that I could bottle it for the future.'

Veronica took a gulp of champagne, waited for the bubbles to stop hurting her chest, then blurted out, 'I kissed him.'

It took so long for Kristin to turn her way she wondered if she'd said the words aloud.

'I mean, I don't think that's why he's a changed man or anything, but I just…I had to tell somebody. I know, I know, I need help. Professional help. I'll understand if you want to disown me. I—'

'Where?' Kristin eventually said, cutting her off mid-babble, and dragging her to a secluded corner of the room behind a pair of life-sized suits of armour.

Veronica blinked. 'On the mouth.'

'No, I mean, when and where did you get the chance to kiss Mitch?'

'After drinks last Friday. He dropped me home. And walked me to my door. And we kissed in front of my apartment. Leading up to the kiss he was a total gentlemen, a tad overprotective perhaps, then it just…kind of happened.'

'*You* kissed Mitch?' Kristin said, still looking almost pale with shock. 'You? A woman with flaws and opinions and years under the bonnet. And he *let* you?'

'Hey!'

Kristin waved a hurried hand across her face. 'That came out wrong. It's just… He's just… You're just… Well, you're not blonde. Or inane. Or three days past your eighteenth birthday. You're, like, cool. And intelligent. And authentic. Yet he didn't run in fear?'

Veronica's chest puffed out. 'Are you suggesting I'm some kind of raging succubus he *ought* to be running away from?'

'No! Of course not.'

'Because I have no desire to nab the guy. It's counterproductive to my cause,' Veronica said, warming up to this venting thing nicely now the valve had been fully released. 'And, besides, he kissed me first.'

Kristin turned to her fully, her face suddenly dead serious. The hairs on the backs of Veronica's arms stood to attention.

'Come on, Kristin, don't look at me like that. I probably shouldn't even have mentioned it. It's so not a big deal. And I'm certain it won't happen again.' She nibbled at her lips for a moment before asking, 'But tell me, how long has Mitch seemed this changed man?'

Kristin looked out across the crowd where their boss was charming a local art dealer. 'Oh, I'd say since about last week just after Friday night. Wow, Veronica, this is huge news.'

'Huge? News? It's hardly either. It was one accidental moment. A moment that I don't plan on allowing to happen again as it surely would not be conducive to a comfortable working relationship. I know, I've been there.'

'The guy on the Gold Coast who's been calling you all week?'

'Geoffrey,' she admitted. 'And before him there was Adam of Sydney Car Sales, who really had seemed like a nice, sensible guy until he ended up on my doorstep in tears because his mother wouldn't let him move out until he was engaged. And Roger the real-estate agent in Adelaide who at my first interview asked if I was married and if I knew how to make a Sunday roast. There's no doubt about it. The time spent looking after Mum left a lingering aura. I attract lonely, desperate men. Not that Mitch is anything like that. Which is why I am so confused.'

Kristin laid a hand over hers. 'Give yourself more credit, my sweet.'

Veronica shrugged off the thought and the sympathy. 'Either way, it's the last thing I want. I'd actually like a job to last longer than six months. I'd like to be in one place long enough to make friends, and find a favourite restaurant and feel as if I belong to something bigger than myself. And I know that kissing the boss isn't the answer.'

Kristin shrugged. 'So those other guys weren't for you. But you said it yourself—it's normal for people to meet their future partners at work. I mean, where else is a girl to meet a guy nowadays? A bar? Online? Tell me, please. I'm having no luck myself.'

Veronica laughed, though it didn't make her feel any better. 'Maybe I am being too hard on the both of us. A fling with a hot, urbane playboy surely never hurt any girl's self-esteem. Even one who puts a dairy-length expiry date on his girlfriends. Perhaps we're made for one another after all.'

She took a sip of champagne, the bubbles mixing uncomfortably with the churning in her stomach. A waiter passed and Veronica put her half-drunk and now-warm drink on the tray.

'No. You're right. It wouldn't work,' she said, even though Kristin hadn't said a word, and even though the minute the words left her mouth the idea grew hooks and claws and refused to let go. 'Better we leave it as a one-off moment and blame the moonlight and cocktails. Time will pass, the embarrassment factor will fade. We'll continue to clash heads over the business, and he'll find another blonde zygote to kiss instead. There. Decided.'

Kristin seemed to listen with only half an ear as she looked over Veronica's shoulder. Without glancing back she knew her friend's eyes were zeroed in on their boss.

'Veronica, honey, I'm trying to tell you, and badly it seems, that I don't think it's quite as simple as you're purporting it to be.'

'Of course it's that simple. Or it can be, at least. Who was that politician's wife who said: Just say no?'

Kristin ignored her lame joke, and rightly so. 'But you like him, don't you?'

'I…' She considered lying outright, wiping her hand across her mouth as if it had been a hardship. But this was Kristin. She let out a long telling sigh. 'Fine. I *like* him. He makes my stomach flutter and my toes curl. Despite the hard head and starched shirts.'

'Well,' Kristin said, 'then I fear I should warn you that, as far as the rumours go you could well be the first flesh and blood woman he's looked at twice since Claire.'

'Who's Claire?'

Kristin bit her lip, and looked at Veronica for the first time in ages. 'Mitch's Claire. I mean… I've told you about her. If not me then somebody. Surely.'

'No,' Veronica said. 'You haven't. Nobody has.'

Kristin suddenly looked anxious, as if she was fighting against the desire to escape. And Veronica felt dread rise up in her throat.

'Kristin, who's Claire?'

'Honey,' Kristin said, planting a comforting hand on Veronica's arm, 'Claire's his wife.'

'Mitch is *married*?' Veronica's voice turned shrill, and when a number of people looked over she grabbed Kristin by the arm and dragged her around the wall's edge to Boris's cluttered, but private and quiet office where her breaths suddenly sounded heavy and laboured.

'He's married?' she asked again.

'Not anymore,' Kristin said, looking more miserable than Veronica thought possible. 'But he was. For about six years. Before I knew him. Actually I think pretty much everyone who knew him back then has been given the chop. Bar Boris and the Hanover House gang who were under his parents' protection at the time he came back to town three years ago.'

'What happened?' Veronica asked, dreading the answer she just knew was coming.

'She died. Suddenly. An aneurism, I think. While they lived in London. He came back here straight after. Went through the company swinging the axe and taking no prisoners. He hired a lot of new blood, including me. And almost overnight he built the business up again, bigger and better. And he hasn't let up since.'

'So the zygote blonde brigade?' Veronica asked, wondering how she could even think of sensible questions as her mind whirled with the awful news.

Kristin smiled, though there was no humour in it. 'They came next. A bevy of arm candy who flit in and out of his BlackBerry so fast I don't know why I bother keying them in in the first place. And then, now, out of the blue, there's you.'

'And then there's me what?'

Kristin placed a dramatic hand over her forehead. 'I feel so stupid! I should have seen it coming. That afternoon after the interview, he was acting all weird and wired up, like he had ants in his pants. Then coming to Friday-night drinks was a shocker. And since then he's seen in the halls whistling to himself. It's all because of you, isn't it?'

Veronica backed up a step until her thighs nudged against the desk so hard it rocked. 'Me? Why me? I haven't done a thing to encourage whistling.'

'Except being your fabulous self.'

She shook her head, hard, until a whip of hair got caught in her eyelash and she had to stop shaking to pull it out. 'Okay, so I was only semi-kidding about the fling-with-a-playboy thing. I am only human. But the *last* thing I want or need is to be the apple of some widower's eye. I came here to get far, far away from that kind of need.'

Kristin shrugged. 'Mitch is the least needy person I've ever met. He's so capable I often wonder why he even keeps me on the payroll. I fear it's for entertainment value more than any service I can provide that he couldn't do himself with both hands tied behind his back. But that doesn't change the fact that you're the first *real* woman who's made an impact since the day I met him.'

Veronica felt a panic attack coming on. 'I haven't made an impact. Not like you mean. It's just...I'm an irritation, an itch some men think they need to scratch until they decide that all that discomfort merely means I'd make the perfect wife.'

Kristin didn't argue, but Veronica could feel her eyes on her all the same. Big dark blue clever eyes taking in every deep breath, every nip at her thumbnail, every rise of her voice.

'He kissed me. Then before tonight he hasn't spoken to me since. So I think you're wrong. I think we can safely assume it was an anomaly. Perhaps all that moonlight made my hair seem fair and he got confused.'

'So we'll choose to ignore the fact that today he brought in lunch for everyone. Eighty people on two floors got free sushi at midday for no reason.'

Oh, God, Veronica thought, slumping her face into her open palms. *Here we go again.*

Though as she focussed on the bright sparks of light flittering through the darkness behind her eyelids she knew the last thing this felt like was more of the same.

This time the man who'd apparently set his sights on her had never looked at her as if he wanted her to tie his ties and cook him dinner. He'd never serenaded her, or bought her flowers or even been particularly nice to her.

He'd kept her on her toes and expected her to prove herself over and over again. And day by day, prod by prod, enigmatic glance by enigmatic glance, she'd found herself wanting to do right by him. Not just herself, or the job, but him. As though his opinion of her mattered that much.

Because she *did* like him. A lot. What was not to like? He was one of the more beautiful creatures allowed to walk the earth. His humour was dry, his personality robust, his presence larger than life. And his kiss… It had melted her from the inside out. She had never, never felt like that in a man's arms before. Loose, willing to let go of the revised grand plan she'd promised herself she'd follow.

But the object of all this misguided affection had been married before. The ache in his eyes, the mask that he used to shut down his palpable charm, was because he was in mourning. And she wasn't willing to cope with the baggage and expectations that he would so clearly bring to any relationship he chose to have. She had enough baggage all of her own.

'So what are you going to do?' Kristin asked, her voice soft. Too soft. As if things were about to fall apart around both of their ears.

'I really, truly have no idea.'

As the night drew to a close and the last of the party attendees drifted out into the spring night Mitch gave into the need that had been escalating inside him all night and sauntered up to Veronica's side.

'What a night,' he said.

She spun, piercing him with a glance so cagey he almost took a step back and raised his hands in surrender. She moved away as she spoke, picking up used napkins and brushing crumbs into her hands.

'You can ease up now, you know,' he said.

'What's the point?' she scoffed. 'Life's short. You gotta live it. Full tilt. Take no prisoners.'

'Sounds exhausting.'

Their eyes locked. Clashed. Hers burned bright with some emotion so turbulent he couldn't pin it down. But he would have had to have been an idiot not to know she wasn't happy. With him.

'Better than standing in the one place for the rest of your life,' she said.

'Meaning?' he asked, the hairs on the back of his neck bristling.

'Meaning I'm wondering what the appeal of the procession of look-alike blondes could possibly be.'

'You said it yourself. Life's short.'

'Right,' she said, her voice dripping with sarcasm.

He had not one clue how their conversation had turned the way it had. He shook his head and chose to change tack himself. 'Can I give you a lift? To my folks' place?'

'Not necessary,' she said, her voice cool, her nose tilted ever so slightly skyward. 'Bar a sip or two of champagne an hour ago I've had nothing but pineapple juice all night. And this time I drove. Lesson learned.'

Lesson? Ah, the other night. She was still glaring at him. Did that mean that for some reason she was angry at him? For the kiss? Or at herself for the same thing? If so, it had taken a while for it to manifest itself. Well, if that was the way she wanted to play it, she was dealing with a guy who could have taken the sport of indifference and gone pro.

He braced his shoulders and glared right on back. 'Do you have the address?'

She nodded.

'Fine, I'll see you there.' With that he turned and left, sparing only a moment to glance over his shoulder, only to find her clenching her fists and rolling her eyes at the ceiling.

And while it ought to have been the perfect antidote to the way she was making him question the heretofore certainty that just the one extraordinary woman had been put on the earth to test and electrify him, her reaction only made him grin. From ear to ear. While his heart thundered in his chest with the power of an astronaut who'd just been told it was his turn to go to the moon.

Boy, oh, boy, had he taken on more than he had foreseen in letting Veronica Bing invade his life.

CHAPTER FIVE

HALF an hour later the Hanovers' butler—yes, *butler*—disappeared into a side room, leaving Veronica to make her way towards the muffled voices at the end of a black-and-white tiled foyer, her eyes wide as they swept every corner of the great room.

'Jeez Louise,' she whispered, craning her neck to take in the moulded murals on the ceiling, furniture far more opulent than anything in the auction house resting unused against discreetly papered walls. Rugs longer than any she'd ever seen ran along the way to what looked to be separate wings of the palatial home.

If Miriam Hanover sold a piece of family art at every auction from here to the year three thousand, the family would still have a lot of nice stuff at their disposal.

The door at the end of the hall was ajar. Still, she knocked before pushing it open, revealing a large yet cosy room packed with overstuffed Wedgwood-blue couches and enough understated lamps to light a small town.

Miriam stood by the working fireplace, stoking a glinting log. A striking silver-haired man remained seated, warming his hands. And Mitch stood in the far corner nursing a drink. The three of them were so refined and beautiful they could have been a subject of a painting in their own auction house.

All the while Veronica found a sudden need to run sweating palms down her tight, bright, sassy red skirt.

'Veronica!' Miriam said, pulling the grate back into place and rushing to her side to give her a familiar kiss on the cheek. 'I've just been dying to introduce you to this handsome fellow over here. This is my husband, Gerald Hanover.'

'Wow,' she said, 'I can see where Mitch gets his good looks.' When the gentleman didn't look like moving, she leant down to shake his hand. 'Lovely to meet you, Gerald.'

'Keep talking like that and I might never let you leave,' he said, pale grey eyes, so very like Mitch's, sparkling in a way Mitch's rarely had.

As to Mitch? He was still looking out over the back yard. His shoulders straight, his neck stiff, his stance upright. She didn't half blame him. After hearing about his circumstances from Kristin she'd gone into a kind of meltdown and likely confused the heck out of him back at the gallery with her talk of blondes and standing still and goodness knew what else she'd blurted at him.

Now, a calming drive in her beloved car later, her own panic abated as her empathy threatened to overcome her. She ached to make some other smart comment to get him to acknowledge her. To notice her. To know she had some idea of what he was going through.

Miriam placed a glass of champagne in her hand and waved at her to sit.

She dragged her attention back to the part of the room that wanted her to be there and sat on the edge of a soft couch, knees together, ankles crossed. 'Miriam, I'd keep my eye on this one,' she said, motioning to Gerald. 'Seems he's a terrible flirt.'

Miriam grinned and sat on the arm of a chair and rested her

hand on her husband's shoulder. 'Don't I know it? I'm not sure if Mitch told you that Gerald and I met working at the gallery.'

At his mother's mentioning of his name finally Mitch came to from wherever he had been. His grey eyes were flat and unreadable in the soft lamplight and Veronica couldn't hope to decipher if Kristin was right. If the short, sweet moments they'd had together in which he'd seemed far more interested in her as a woman than as an employee were as fraught with peril as she'd thought they would have to be.

'He owned the place,' Miriam continued, 'and I was hired on Reception. It was love at first sight, for him anyway. And he spent the next several months asking me out every day until I agreed to go on one date.'

'Best decision I ever made,' Gerald said.

'Please. This from a man who took a small family business and imagined the makings of an empire,' Miriam said.

'You're a romantic, aren't you, Gerald?' Veronica said.

'You bet I am.'

'That's a rarer quality than you might imagine.'

'Oh, I don't know,' Miriam said. 'I think most men have it in them, they just need the right woman to bring it out.' Her soft blue gaze shot her son's way and Veronica saw a shaft of something akin to pain shoot across her expression.

She pinched herself in the thigh in punishment for being far less subtle than she'd hoped to be. It would pay to remember that her boss came from a family of smart, sharp-minded people. Who'd been hurt by the loss of a daughter-in-law. And weren't over it yet.

'Aren't you planning on defending our sex, son?' Gerald asked.

Mitch had taken up residence just behind Veronica. Close enough she could smell the last remaining wafts of his aftershave. Close enough her bare arms prickled as the hairs stood on end. Close enough she didn't dare turn to face him lest he see in her eyes all she now knew about him. About the reason behind his sadness, why he surrounded himself with women who didn't challenge him. About Claire.

Though not so much about why he'd gone against his recent nature and kissed *her*…

'I don't know how much defending we can do without looking ridiculous,' Mitch said, his low voice reverberating through her bones. 'Don't you know they take these girls aside in high school, and teach them just where to kick us where it hurts most—right in our perfectly respectable macho camouflage?'

Veronica raised her glass to her lips and took a long slow sip. She smiled at Gerald as she said, 'You men just need to know there's no need for camouflage. A little casual, innocent, momentary lapse into romance never hurt anyone.'

When she didn't turn to face him, Mitch moved, easing around the back of the couch to take a seat in a tub chair on the other side of the elegant cream French provincial coffee-table so that she had no choice but to meet his gaze.

'So you think we fellas ought to shout out how we feel, loud and proud?' Mitch said, his grey eyes unexpectedly dancing. 'Damn the consequences?'

Okay, so that wasn't what she'd meant at all. She'd meant to let him off the hook.

'Of course you should,' Gerald said when she'd been quiet for too long. 'If you go for broke and get rejected, you're no worse off than you were before, and if you get a yes, well, then, your life will never be the same again. Don't you think, Veronica?'

Veronica's heart picked up the same rhythm as the light dancing in Mitch's eyes, performing a pretty darned tricky rumba against her ribs. Treading carefully, she said, 'Well, along the same lines, if I hadn't presented myself as the answer to your prayers, I have the funny feeling you wouldn't have given me the job.'

Miriam laughed. As did Gerald. Mitch merely twinkled her way all the harder while she silently begged him to stop.

'You really think that?' he asked.

She nodded, her throat now too dry to find any clever words.

'Is that true?' Gerald asked.

Mitch sat forward in his chair and his mouth turned up in that slow, sexy smile of his. 'Being that I am of a more taciturn nature than my dramatic dear old dad, I guess we'll never know.'

'Balderdash. Veronica, all Mitch has done since he got home tonight is sing your praises.'

Mitch's eyes remained firmly on hers as he sipped at his drink. No frothy, fun, celebratory champagne for him. His crystal-cut glass was swimming in a centimetre of some dark spirit that no doubt matched his own. But he hadn't been there when Kristin had spilled the beans. He was blithely unaware how much Veronica now knew.

She realised then that, so long as she kept things breezy and light, this so far pleasant evening with his parents acting as inadvertent chaperons might well be her opportunity to turn the tide and get everything back to a simple boss-employee relationship.

'This Mitch?' she said, smiling for the first time since she'd entered the intimidating house now that she felt as if she wasn't the one who was outnumbered. 'Singing my praises? Tell me more.'

'Well,' Gerald said, 'Miriam was telling me about your speech, and Mitch went on to say how you... How did you put it, Mitch?'

'Yeah, Mitch. How did you put it?' She fully expected Mitch to baulk, or fend or stay silent. To hide behind *macho camouflage*.

But instead, he placed his drink on the table, let his hands rest relaxedly atop his thighs and said, 'I may have mentioned that in all my years of working as a dogsbody at Hanover House as a kid, of being dragged along to auctions as a recalcitrant teen, before I finally fled the country to avoid having to show my face at every show through adulthood, I had never before seen anyone have clients eating out of the palms of their hands as easily as you did tonight.'

And then he said, 'You were quite something out there tonight.'

'Surprised?'

'Not in the least.'

She clamped tight to her glass to stop anyone from seeing that her hands had begun to shake. Because even though they were talking business, Mitch Hanover, widower, boss, fabulous kisser, was right then telling her how he felt, loud and proud as a man encrusted in macho camouflage could. So much for it turning out to be no more than a pleasant evening….

'That smells as if dinner's ready,' Miriam said, her voice blithe and happy as she stood and looked towards a door at the far end of the room. 'Shall we?'

God, yes. Veronica slowly put her glass on the table.

Miriam moved behind her husband's chair and began to push. And only then did Veronica even notice that beneath the fine angora rug tossed over his knees his chair had wheels.

Mitch stood. She had to crane her neck to look up at him. He eased over to her, holding out a hand to her. She took it and let him pull her to her feet.

First Claire and now this? No wonder he's so closed off.

'Please tell me your father is all right,' she whispered.

'He had a motorcycle accident many years ago,' he murmured so close to her ear she felt her hair tickle against her neck. 'He'll outlive us all.'

When she didn't move a hair, he lightly placed her hand in the crook of his arm and laughed softly, sending her taut nerves into meltdown.

'Relax, Veronica. I promise the next hour won't hurt a bit.'

Veronica bit back a manic laugh. Who was he to tell her how she was going to get out of this evening unscathed? She was enamoured of his mother, besotted by his darling father, and with every passing minute she felt more and more deeply attached to him.

Mitch was as much of a survivor as she was, and, rather than making her feel delighted that she had actually met a man truly able to take care of himself, it only made her want to wipe his brow, and rub his feet and make everything all better.

And as he walked her through the double French doors and into the dining room, with the scent of his aftershave swirling in her nostrils, the feel of his warm, strong body knocking against hers, and the hum of his deep suggestive voice ringing in her ears, she felt herself warming to the idea that he might be the kind of man who'd be able to make her feel all better too.

She looked to the moulded ceiling and whispered, 'Heaven help me.'

'Did you say something?' Mitch asked.

'Oh, nothing. Nothing at all.'

Light supper was followed by a decadent dessert. And Mitch watched in mute fascination as Veronica polished off the lot without one word as to what it might do to her hips.

He found himself wondering how deeply meditative his

waking state must have been these past few years to have survived so many women who'd eaten like sparrows, thinking it
would actually impress him. The thought made him feel a tad
foolish.

'So, Gerry,' Veronica said, wiping a finger into the leftover
chocolate sauce and licking it off with pure delight in her eyes,
'how did you get this gorgeous wife of yours to finally crack?
Did you buy her flowers every day? Propose every other week?
Sky-write her name over Melbourne?'

Gerald leant forward and whispered conspiratorially. 'I
cornered her in the kitchenette and gave her the best kiss of her
young life.'

At his father's previously unheard tale, Mitch's backbone
sprung dead straight so quickly he almost pulled a muscle. He
looked to his mother, who was grinning from ear to ear, and
blushing like mad. While Veronica's shocked laughter cracked
boisterously through the large room, echoing off the walls long
after it subsided to an indulgent smile.

Veronica rested an elbow on the table and her chin on her
upturned palm and glanced from Miriam to Gerald. 'That must
have been some kiss.'

Her eyes were dancing, her voice light, but Mitch noticed
she hadn't once looked his way since that word had been mentioned. He didn't half blame her. The coincidences were piling
up around them so fast he found himself gripping on to his linen
napkin for dear life.

'Gerry,' Veronica said, her voice just husky enough Mitch
had to shuffle in his seat to dissipate the sudden blood rush to
his centre.

'Yes, Veronica,' his father said, voice rich with flirtation.

'Nowadays that would be classed as sexual harassment.'

Miriam laughed and put a soothing hand over her husband's.

'She's right, you know. I could have sued and made millions. But that would have taken the fun out of things, don't you think?'

Veronica picked up her glass of iced water. 'I'll drink to that!'

'Hear, hear,' Gerald said, raising his glass and noisily clinking hers.

Miriam did the same, her effortless delight reminding Mitch of how it used to be before he'd come home from London. Had it really been that long since he'd heard his mother laugh? Had his self-imposed emotional exile made that wide an impact?

Veronica's glass suddenly appeared before him, and for the first time since the main meal began her gaze locked with his. She held her glass aloft. Was she encouraging him to salute the idea of more kissing in the workplace? He looked deep into her soft brown eyes, wondering just what she was playing at.

'Aren't you going to toast, boss? Just think, if your father had been more backward about coming forward you wouldn't be here.'

Mitch leant forward, holding her gaze. When her glass dropped an inch and her resolute gaze began to waver he lifted his glass. 'Then how could I possibly refuse?'

Their glasses touched, the zing ricocheting down his arm and into his funny bone. Their gazes held for just a split second longer before she blinked, frowned, shook her head ever so slightly, then turned away to take a sip.

Six months, he thought, and not for the first time, *is nothing like for ever*.

'You're a plucky young woman, Ms Bing,' his father said.

She smiled easily at his father as she said, 'A woman after your own heart, I would think, Mr Hanover.'

Gerald Hanover winked at her in return.

'Are you seeing this?' Mitch said in a quiet aside to his mother.

Miriam nodded furiously. Her voice was slightly hoarse as she whispered, 'Doesn't it feel like if she told him to get up and walk, he'd actually try?'

Mitch leant back away, knowing his mother had hit the nail on the head. Veronica's liveliness was infectious. She was like a magnet drawing in lost souls who wanted to know what it felt like to live with even one hundredth of her boundless energy.

But it was more than that. She was more than that.

His father had been in a wheelchair for twenty-odd years yet even some of his closest friends still treated him with kid gloves. While this relative stranger was treating him with as much irreverence and spunk as if he was the bull of a man he had once been.

She was a revelation.

'Wherever did you find her?' Gerald said, turning to Mitch, his pale eyes gleaming with good humour.

Mitch took the opportunity to have a long, invited look at their dinner companion. 'Would you believe she simply turned up on my doorstep one day?'

His father smiled. 'I'd believe it, and if I were you, I'd thank my lucky stars for it every single day.'

His lucky stars?

The answer to all his dreams?

If he were a romantic, he might begin to believe in the kind words of his friends and family. But it had been some time since the romantic inside him had been brutally chopped away. Holding Claire's hand, his face wet with tears as she had slipped away in her hospital bed, had wrenched any last romantic notions from his existence.

'We'll wait and see how the auction goes,' he said, needing to temper his parents' verve as much as his own. 'Bring that off, Ms Bing, and we'll all be thanking our lucky stars, our chakras and any gods who might be smiling kindly upon us at the time.'

Veronica smiled, her glossy lips stretching across her face, her head tilting ever so slightly to one side as she acknowledged the hit. She raised her glass again, this time only to him, the thrill of the challenge gleaming in her bright eyes.

So much for dampening any connection he felt with the woman. All that glittering energy only served to rekindle long since forgotten warm places deep inside him to the point where his lungs felt as if they were about to burn him from the inside out.

And right there, sitting at his parents' dining table, on an otherwise insignificant Wednesday night in spring, for the first time in a long time, the romantic inside of him began to itch like a phantom limb.

After a dinner in which Veronica smiled so much she thought her face might split in two, the boys retired to the sitting room. While Miriam snuck a hand in the crook of Veronica's arm and dragged her off down a long hall to 'show off her tapestries'.

Veronica wouldn't know a tapestry from a rug, but she went along happily. Some time away from Mitch's piercing grey gaze would do her breath some good.

She and Miriam had barely made it ten metres down the hall when Miriam asked, 'So what do you think of my Mitch?'

Oh, heck, Veronica thought. Her cheeks heated uncomfortably as she said, 'I'm sure I don't know him well enough to have an informed opinion.'

'Your uninformed opinion will do,' Miriam said hopefully.

'Right. Then he seems an astute and dedicated businessman.'
Excellent, beautifully deflected.

Miriam drew her into a side room, which turned out to be a

small library. With its fifteen-foot ceilings and wall-to-wall shelves filled with books it could have been a seriously imposing room, but with the surfeit of light wood furniture and cream couches it was as inviting as the rest of the large house.

She looked up from the sweet furnishings to find Miriam pacing in the middle of the room wringing her hands.

Veronica mentally kicked herself, wondering what she could have said wrong this time. 'Miriam?'

Miriam glanced up, her eyes troubled as she dredged up a watery smile. 'I'm hardly playing the role of gracious hostess, am I?'

Veronica moved towards her, arm out, but not quite knowing what to do. She barely knew this woman. True, she barely knew the woman's son, either, yet could have found a hundred better words to describe what she really thought of him than 'astute' and 'dedicated'.

Miriam sat. Veronica picked out a soft wing-chair and did the same. She searched for something to say to lighten the mood. But Miriam got in first.

'He's just been so different since he came home from London.' Miriam shook her head and scrunched up her eyes. 'Of course he has. After what happened with Claire. I only mean that, when he came home, he wasn't just sorrowful, he was also no longer the sweet, loving, generous boy I'd always known. There's a frostiness about him now that I don't know how to get past.'

Veronica didn't know what to say. This night was turning out to be one of the more emotionally topsy-turvy of her already chequered life. She could have feigned ignorance. She could have shrugged and said, 'I dunno.' But with Miriam sitting there looking so wretched, her compassion came out of hiding.

'Claire was his wife, right?' she said.

Miriam glanced up, and shook her head again, but this time her smile was truer. 'I'm sorry. I shouldn't have even brought it up. It's just you've fit in so beautifully I'd forgotten you're only newly with us. Most of the Hanover House staff have been part of the family almost as long as I have, but Mitch has had so little to do with them since coming home.'

'It's okay,' Veronica said. 'Maybe that's why it's easier to talk to me. For all intents and purposes I am still an outsider.'

She tucked a hand over Miriam's, warming to her far more quickly than it was usual for her to warm to anyone. She wasn't silly, she knew it was because Miriam was of a certain age, a certain temperament and had taken a certain interest in her. Having a mother figure was powerful stuff.

She took a breath and reminded herself she had a six-month contract with a business on the verge of falling apart. There was no point making the kinds of connections her subconscious was craving for her to make. With *any* of the Hanover family. She was only setting herself up for a huge fall.

But she couldn't let this nice woman sit there looking so sad. 'So you want to know my impressions of Mitch.'

Miriam looked to her as if she were about to impart the secrets of life, the universe and everything. And just as if she were talking to her own mother Veronica wanted so badly not to disappoint.

She took a deep breath, collected her thoughts and said, 'I've found him to be, by turns, charming, unexpected, difficult, stubborn, funny, hard-nosed, kind and a real live gentleman.'

She thought it kinder to leave out that she too had been on the receiving end of an icy blast or two. For Miriam it would no doubt be heartbreaking. But for Veronica it had made the moments when she had for some reason been allowed to see beneath the reserve to the good stuff beneath all that more significant.

She also left out the fact that she found him sexy as hell. For obvious reasons.

As Miriam digested her words her expression went from solemn, to hopeful, to far too understanding. Her eyes filled with such hope Veronica knew she needed to shoot it down before the poor woman put all her hopes on Veronica's shoulders. She knew from experience that kind of pressure would only make her want to cut and run.

And after the challenge, and the terror and the final success of the pre-show, she knew she wasn't yet ready to leave. There was more she could offer the place. And more it could offer her.

'Don't get too excited, though,' Veronica said, pointing a finger at Miriam's nose. 'As a boss he can be a stuck-in-the-mud pain in the proverbial you know what.'

Miriam laughed, and brushed a finger under one eye. Veronica's heart went out to her. And to her gorgeous husband who doted on his son just as obviously.

She found herself intensely wishing her own parents were still around. She wished they'd been there tonight to see how far she'd come. She wished they'd been around long enough for her to make them as proud as Mitch's parents were of him.

'So you don't think him a lost cause?' Miriam asked.

'Not completely. Especially when he has you lot to keep him level-headed.'

Miriam drew herself to her feet, then took both of Veronica's hands and pulled her standing also. 'I've asked far too much of you. You'll think it's why I invited you here when I simply wanted to welcome you to the Hanover House family.'

'Then you've done your job. I feel as welcome as can be,' Veronica promised.

A maid in an old-fashioned black-and-white uniform came

quietly into the room. 'The phone, Ms Miriam,' she said. 'Paula Jenkinson.'

Miriam let Veronica's hands go. 'Did you meet Paula tonight?'

Veronica shook her head.

'You will soon enough. She's one of our favourite customers. And she'll be calling with her opinion about tonight's show. And about you too, my dear.'

Miriam placed her cool hand on Veronica's cheek as she looked deep into her eyes. And then she turned and left, leaving Veronica feeling as though she'd somehow done good.

Not quite sure what she was meant to do now, she took a tour of the room. Books lined the walls, as did so many family photos she wondered if any had been left to collect dust in locked-away albums.

One framed picture made her feet come to a staggering halt. A photo of Mitch. His dark hair was still short but less structured. His handsome face more filled out. The top two buttons of his white shirt dashingly unbuttoned. And he was in the arms of a beautiful auburn-haired waif who was shoving wedding cake into his mouth.

She took the picture from the shelf and ran her finger across both faces. They looked deliriously happy. As if they had the world at their feet and were chomping at the bit to take it on. And were very much in love.

Veronica's heart took a little tumble. She had to hold a hand to her chest to quell the ache. If Mitch Hanover had it in him to love that deeply, to be that happy, and that carefree, no wonder his mother was heartbroken that he hid all that potential inside the outer shell of a hard-headed businessman with time only for fleeting relationships.

Was he no more than a shell of the man he'd once been? Was

that because they had been so much in love one couldn't live without the other? She'd seen it happen with her parents. She knew it wasn't a mythical kind of love. It could happen.

Her gaze went back to Mitch's image and became stuck. There was no doubting the depths of his love for his wife. Her breaths grew shallow as she dropped her hand, opened her chest and giddily allowed herself to imagine how it might feel to have that man look at her in that way. And for a woman who'd done her all to remain untouched and independent, the sudden rampant desire to be so cherished was heady indeed.

A knock at the French windows leading to the back yard made her jump and turn. Mitch was standing outside.

She quickly hid the photo behind her back, desperately hoping he hadn't been standing there too long.

With a slight tilt of his head he motioned for her to join him, then he moved away and disappeared into the darkness.

Veronica took several deep breaths before gently putting the photograph back where it belonged. She straightened her clothes, ran a shaking hand over her hair, licked her dry lips, then did as she was asked and went to join the man who was fast turning her from a happily self-sustaining individual into a walking basket-case.

CHAPTER SIX

THE air outside the Hanover family house was a few degrees cooler, but Veronica found her body was already adapting to being back home.

Home? She looked around her. This wasn't like any home she'd ever known. The cluttered, three-bedroom, one-bathroom, brick-veneer suburbia of her youth had made way for minimalist, everything-must-be-able-to-fit-into-a-suitcase, apartment living. While this place was like something out of *The Great Gatsby*.

A double tennis court was lit by discreet shrub lamps to the right, a high rendered wall kept the rest of the world at bay to the left and right in front a large kidney-shaped swimming pool was surrounded with mature palms and masses of bougainvillea spilling over beautifully arranged rocks.

'There I was blithely thinking all sales jobs were the same,' she said, her tense voice fast disappearing into the wide-open space. 'I never imagined I'd find myself hanging out in a place like this or getting graded by septuagenarian poodles.'

'Excuse me?'

She turned to Mitch, who was standing in the shadows. After her recent conversations with Kristin and Miriam she'd decided he did it on purpose. It was all part of hiding from the lighter side of life.

'Your mother is right now on the phone with Paula Jenkinson. Should I be worried?'

'If Paula didn't have an opinion, then I'd be worried.'

She nodded, and moved towards the pool, which was twinkling with something other than the stars above. Looking up, she found the source of the twinkling: a hundred minuscule fairy lights curled in among the ivy growing over the criss-cross pergola roof above her.

She crouched to dip her finger in the surprisingly warm water.

'It's heated,' Mitch said.

'Of course it is.' She stood, flicked water onto the tiles, then rubbed her hands down her bare arms.

'Don't tell me you're cold again.'

'Not cold. Just on a little refinement overload.'

'You seem as if you're coping fine to me.'

Coping? Perhaps that was the perfect word for how she felt. Or muddling through. Hanging on to her confidence, and to her usually so guarded heart, by her fingernails.

'When I worked the comic-book conventions in Sydney,' she said, dropping the volume of her voice to match the quiet night, 'I had guys called Larry and Angus following me around like groupies, begging me to tell them which Superman comic was my favourite. And when I worked the used-car auctions in Brisbane, I had guys with tattoos and piercings assuming I actually knew what a carburettor was. They didn't faze me a bit. But here…this place is far more daunting than I imagined it would be.'

A creaking sound behind her had her looking over her shoulder to find Mitch had taken up residence upon a white slatted wood daybed. He was lying back with arms behind his head as he looked up at the blanket of stars above. 'That's another thing I ought to apologise for.'

'What's that?'

'I haven't exactly been all that forthcoming with support.'

She could have fobbed him off. Feigned nonchalance. But after all she'd been through this day she couldn't be bothered. 'No,' she said. 'You really haven't.'

At that he glanced over at her, his grey eyes steely and shrouded. 'You're not in the least bit intimidated by me, are you?'

'Intimidated? No.' *Intrigued, smitten, infatuated, confused, torn. You bet.* 'You may be a big guy, but the used-car sales regulars had a good twenty kilos on you.'

Mitch smiled; she felt it sliding to her through the darkness until it settled upon her cheek like a kiss. Her heart lurched. She slumped down onto the edge of the matching white daybed next to his.

'So how did you get into auctioneering?' he asked.

She glanced at him, looking for his angle. Her eyes narrowed. 'Are you still interviewing me?'

His smile turned into a laugh. The image of him and his wife on their wedding day slammed into her mind and she wondered what kind of strength it had taken to find laughter again.

He said, 'Not at all. I really want to know.'

'If you're looking for a fun anecdote I can tell you about the time I sent Larry and Angus on a wild-goose chase for the little-known—meaning completely made up—comic in which it was revealed Spiderman is actually gay—'

He laughed again. Softer. Gentler. Indulging her. 'Maybe later. Right now I want to know what brought you here.'

'Fine. Fine. I was studying business at university and that's where I met Kristin. But I had to quit late in my first year. My father had passed away and within six weeks my mother was diagnosed with Alzheimer's. She was in her mid-sixties.'

She stopped to take a breath. Mitch didn't aim to fill the silence, but he did sit up. For a moment she was sure he was going to reach out to her, but his hands tucked around the edges of the chair keeping three feet and two lifetimes of difficult experiences as a crevice between them.

She kept her eyes dead ahead then, focussed on the lights dancing across the shimmering pool water. 'During the time I took care of Mum I became involved with the Australian Alzheimer's Association, working to fundraise for Alzheimer's research. I had no fear asking for what our charity wanted even when those with the power didn't necessarily want to give it to me.'

'And you were how old?' Mitch asked, his deep voice wafting to her on the mild evening breeze.

'I was just twenty when Mum passed. Then I was suddenly thrust into the real world with no experience, no training, no degree, completely unemployable compared with others my age unless I wanted to flip burgers for a living. So when the Australian Alzheimer's Association roped me into running the auction at their first fundraising ball, I leapt at the chance to feel useful. I did it, loved it and have done the same every year since. Oh, shoot,' she said, spinning to face Mitch, 'I should have mentioned that in the interview. My work for them goes against the exclusivity agreement I signed with you. And it means I need a week off in November to go to Sydney.'

Oh, heck, if he told her no…she had no idea what she'd do. *Quit?* After all the work she'd done redecorating the gallery, giving the Hanover House staff hope? And then there was…

'Mitch, I don't want to beg, but—'

'Stop fretting,' he said, and this time nothing stopped him from reaching out. His large hand clasped hers, enveloping it in warmth and strength, and the three feet between them felt like three millimetres. 'I'm not a complete tyrant. You can have the time off. You can still run their auction. I had no idea I had an ideological warrior on my hands.'

Her hand shifted so that it fitted more fully inside his. 'Hardly. I owe them for the help they gave Mum and me. Nothing more.'

His mouth curved into a slow smile. 'And with that magnanimous spirit guiding you, of all the places you could have worked in this wide brown land you chose Hanover House. I feel honoured.'

She realised then he was still holding her hand. In fact, his thumb was now stroking the inside of her palm. So slowly, so gently, she wasn't even sure he knew he was doing it. But *she* knew. She moaned blissfully on the inside as he massaged tense spots she hadn't even known she'd had.

She managed to mumble something like, 'It felt like time to come home. And when Kristin put out the word, it seemed a perfect fit.'

'I'm not sure what kind of looking-glass the two of you had, but I took some convincing of that.'

'Now that I've seen the kinds of people who frequent your shows you must have thought I'd stepped out of the circus.' She laughed. 'Heck, when I think about how I was dressed...'

She glanced up at him, still feeling the smile warming her. But her smile faded when she came smack against the look in his eyes.

Kristin said she'd never seen Mitch happy like regular people could be happy. His mother worried that he had surrounded himself by a wall of protective ice that might never be melted.

And, though right in that moment he didn't exactly look happy, the ache she'd sensed in him was missing too.

His eyes had darkened, the twitch in his cheek that she seemed to bring on like some kind of tic had settled, his breaths were slow and even. And he was looking at her as if regret was the last thing on his mind. He was looking at her as if he wanted to kiss her again. More than kiss her. He was looking at her with hope.

He turned her hand over and the strokes became deeper, more purposeful. He glanced down, his dark eyes burning every centimetre of bare skin they touched on the way.

Moonlight spilled around them like fairy dust. Again she found herself so drawn to him. Despite all her very sensible reasons not to let this simmering attraction between them go a step further, she would have given her right foot to kiss him too.

And if she had been the kind of girl to go there with a co-worker once or twice before, she'd had good reason: bereavement, then misguided attraction and finally loneliness. Now she was older and wiser she'd learned her lesson. Hadn't she?

She slid her hand from his. Naked to the cool spring night, it grew pins and needles until she rubbed warmth back into the poor dejected thing. But he reached out and took her hand again, this time holding it between both of his.

She looked up from where their hands were intertwined and into his beautifully etched face. Her heart fluttered. Her stomach clenched. And she finally admitted to herself that what she felt for Mitch Hanover went way beyond excuses or reason of any kind.

'Mitch,' she said, her voice husky as all get out.

'Yes, Veronica.'

'What are you doing?'

'What does it feel like I'm doing?'

'I'm trying really hard not to come to any conclusions.'

'What if I told you that I haven't been able to stop thinking about our kiss?'

Okay. So he'd said it. He'd mentioned the kiss. It was out there now, hovering between them like a loaded bomb, the ticking of which matched the fast pace of her heart.

'Then I'd think you were now trying to seduce me.'

'Should I keep trying?'

His gaze lifted from her hand, slunk along her arm, paused briefly on her bare neck, then meandered slowly, achingly slowly, up her face. When his eyes met hers her breath was sapped completely from her lungs and she was glad to be sitting down as in that moment her knees completely forgot how they were meant to work.

'If that's why you hired me, Mitch, if you think I'm some kind of indiscriminate, easy, breezy beach chick you can entice into three dates then brush off with a bunch of flowers bought by Kristin, then you can think again.'

Even in the muted light she could see his neck pink, and the muscles around his mouth contract. Either he was embarrassed about being sprung or was thinking of a way to punish Kristin come the morning. Her reaching heart hoped it might be the first, her lucid brain feared it was the second.

'I don't think of you that way, Veronica,' he said. And once again her name on his lips made her melt.

'So you're telling me you don't have some funny idea that I'm an uncomplicated blonde in disguise.'

'Not for a second.'

'Okay, then.'

Okay, then? So what was he saying? What was he offering? Five dates? Six if she was lucky? A month to worship at the altar of Mitch Hanover, stud muffin extraordinaire, before he came to his senses and cast her aside?

She swallowed. 'This is probably as good a time as any to let you know that you can cut out the act. I know that deep down you're no raging playboy, either.'

His left eyebrow rose. It was so incredibly sexy she had to bite her lip to stop herself from leaning over to kiss it.

'Me? Not a playboy? And whatever gave you that idea?'

She took a deep shaky breath. What she said next would alter the course of their relationship for ever. It might send him scurrying deeper inside his cave. Or heaven forbid it might bring them closer. But she said it anyway. 'The fact that you've had a Claire in your life.'

As soon as the words left her mouth she felt him retreating. He let her go, his eyes lost their spark, his skin lost all colour, and his large, broad, strong, capable body seemed to slump inside itself.

'My mother told you,' he said, his voice ragged where only seconds before it had been brimming with sexual confidence.

Not wanting to get his mother or Kristin into any more strife, she said, 'A workplace is like a small community, Mitch. Everybody knows everybody else's business. Or if they don't, they soon will.'

His head lowered into his hands. Her empathy, which had been bubbling beneath the surface, shot through the cracks in her heart like a volcano. She had to do something to make him feel less as though he were alone in the spotlight.

She took a deep breath and said, 'The real reason I left the Gold Coast, and my previous job, is because of my relationship with my last boss.'

Mitch didn't flinch. Didn't even seem to take a breath. So she simply went on.

'It never went further than a couple of innocent dates. Geoffrey would have preferred my decision to have been different and did everything in his power to make it so. As such everyone else in the computer-game intellectual-property biz on the Coast assumed it was a *fait accompli* and judged me accordingly. I was talked about behind my back. Shunned for sleeping my way into the job. When he didn't do anything to assuage the rumours that we were hot and heavy, I had no choice but to leave. So there it is. The real reason I'm here.'

It was a few moments before Mitch ran his hands over his face and looked back at her. By that stage he'd found a way out of the darkness and was sitting taller, straighter, almost the epitome of the cool, collected, together man. Almost.

'Geoffrey sounds like a schmuck,' he said.

Veronica laughed, which was the last thing she'd expected to do, relief pouring through her like the first sip of a fine wine. 'Yeah. He was all that and more.'

'Yet I can't blame the guy.'

She blinked. 'I sure can.'

'But then I'm fairly sure you don't see the things in yourself that others do. That Kristin did. That my parents do. Hell, even the schmuck knew what he had at his fingertips.'

The together man was now more than together. Mitch was looking her dead in the eye, holding her gaze with nothing more than the sheer force of his personality.

She searched the air for Claire's shadow, but all she could feel was a light breeze ruffling her hair. All she could smell was nearby potted gardenias. All she could hear was the steady thrum of her heartbeat. And all she could see was the man sitting before her, looking at her as if *she* were a spectre who had appeared to him out of the darkness.

He knew her secret shame. She knew his secret pain. Yet the attraction still crackled between them like the heralding of a wildfire.

'What can you see?' she asked.

He lifted a hand to her cheek then, tucking a curl behind her ear. 'That you're not afraid of anything.'

'Me?' she said, slapping herself on the chest and fast losing her hand within a wave of black ruffles. 'Not afraid? Wherever did you get that idea?'

'I've never met anyone as sure-footed as you are. From the moment you walked through the door of my gallery, you've known every single step you planned to take to get to this point.'

Veronica's next bout of laughter was slightly hysterical. Though she was talking with her boss about business, and appearing sure-footed was probably a good thing, while he played with her hair and looked deep into her eyes she hadn't felt less sure-footed in her entire life.

'Don't believe everything you see, Mitch. To be a great salesperson one also has to be an accomplished actor.'

His face creased into the kind of smile any girl would feel lucky to be on the receiving end of: gentle, intimate and all for her. He said, 'And to reach the kind of success I have a person has to be a good judge of character.'

Veronica shook her head and reached up to pull his hand away from where it had begun sliding hypnotically around the back of her neck. She brought their hands to her lap, this time holding on to him. She closed her eyes for a second.

Help! How can I put this right before it spins further out of control?

She opened her eyes and gave him every bit of honesty she could muster. No sales pitch, no smoke and mirrors, just the God's honest truth. 'You have me so wrong, Mitch. Right now, right this second, sitting out here, with you, I'm actually fairly petrified.'

'Of what?'

Oh, heck. What does a girl have to do to get a freak earthquake right when she needs one?

'Of you,' she said. 'And me. And of allowing the magic of nights like this mean more in my head than they would in the harsh light of day.'

'Veronica—'

'Uh-uh. I'm nowhere near finished. I'm terrified of the thought of you kissing me again. And just as terrified that you might never kiss me again. I'm rattled by Claire. Petrified that Geoffrey and his ilk will hound me the rest of my natural life. But most of all, I'm scared witless that if I do what I know I ought to and stand up right now and bid you goodnight and avoid you like the plague for the next five and a bit months, I'll regret it for the rest of my life.'

After she'd finished, her next breaths in and out were so shaky she wondered if they gave away the depth of her confusion even more than her words had.

Mitch's eyes grew dark, but his right cheek kicked into a smile. And had he moved closer? The moonlight had shifted and his face was in stark relief. She could see the flecks of a thousand different colours in his deep eyes.

His hand moved so that he could run his thumb along her bottom lip, tugging the skin and creating skitters of building awareness.

And then he said, 'So don't walk away.'

'Ha! You make it sound so simple.'

'I like simple.'

Pity then that letting anything happen with Mitch Hanover would be anything but.

Mitch's gaze dropped, and he took in a deep slow breath as it grazed her mouth, which dropped open so that she too could draw in deeper breaths.

He was going to kiss her again, of this she had no doubt. And she was going to let him. Despite her own growing feelings, despite the fact that he was her boss, despite the fact that his current idea of a meaningful relationship was a cocktail, a one-sided conversation and a cab home.

Maybe that was the answer right there. Maybe she should get over her hang-ups and just let it happen. Then he'd move on as he always did and, since they knew where they stood from the outset, there would be no hard feelings.

They could both have what they obviously wanted. Nobody else had to know. Nobody had to get hurt. It was win-win.

Veronica swallowed down the hot mixture of very real fear and excitement throbbing through her intoxicated veins. She didn't look away. She couldn't. He watched her right on back. And it didn't feel like the beginning of cocktails, a one-sided conversation and a cab home.

It felt more serious. And far bigger than her limited experience with such feelings had her prepared for. That was the most frightening moment of her day yet.

She found herself in sudden need of the comfort of sameness. Of her own space. Of time alone in her head without this sensory invasion. Of the wind in her hair and white noise filling her ears while she sat encased in two tonnes of hot-pink American engineering, which was thankfully awaiting her in the driveway.

'Mitch,' she said, before she had to take a second to clear her throat. 'It's been a crazy night and I'm sure we're both still running on the high of success. Perhaps it would be for the best if I just got going.'

After a long charged pause during which he looked deep into her eyes, his thoughts flitting too fast for her to catch a one, he said, 'Yeah. You're probably right.'

He stood, blocking out the moonlight so that she looked up

to the broadest male form she'd ever seen. He held out a hand. She took it. Warm, long fingers closed tight around hers, tugging her to her feet until her chest brushed against his, so close she could feel it expanding with each deep breath.

Veronica said, 'I'd better go and find your parents and thank them for the lovely dinner. No doubt they'll be wondering what happened to us.'

For whatever reason, that fact alone was enough for Mitch to finally let her go. He rubbed a hand hard through the back of his hair and pulled away, physically and emotionally. He glanced up at their surrounds, surprise lighting his eyes. 'You know, I'd forgotten we were even here.'

She felt she needed to say more, to redraw the boundaries between them more clearly than the last time they'd parted, so in the end she went with, 'Thank you for this opportunity, Mitch. Truly. I really am loving working at Hanover House, and not just for the chance to persuade lovely people like Paula Jenkinson and Bernie Walden to part with their cash.'

He smiled as he was meant to, but the earlier light she had seen within him had dimmed. It pained her to see it gone, but it also gave her the strength to say what needed to be said.

'The work, the working relationships, the goodwill I have fostered in the art-collecting community are things I don't want to jeopardise. I've made friends here. And I hope I can count you as one of them.'

After a few moments he gave her one short nod. Nothing more. But it was enough for her to feel as though she'd been given some space. Some time. Some relief.

Pleasantries exhausted, lines reconstructed, she stepped forward, held out her hand for a shake, then pulled it back in when that felt just silly. Finally she leant in, placed a hand on his shoulder and kissed him on the cheek.

His scent enveloped her as though it had merely been waiting for its chance. She closed her eyes for a fraction of a second, memorised the texture of his cheek, the light kiss of his hair against her nose, then she pulled away and walked away without looking back.

CHAPTER SEVEN

Mitch's office phone rang. He snapped it to his ear. 'Yes?'

There followed a pause long enough for him to look up from the contract strewn across his large desk to frown across the room.

He glanced at his watch. Midday, and he hadn't eaten since the double espresso Kristin had forced upon him when he'd first arrived. And was it Thursday? Was it that late in the day and that late in the week already? He swore beneath his breath.

'Yes?' he said again, this time not even trying to hide his exasperation that he'd been bothered. But who was he kidding? He'd felt permanently bothered all morning.

'Mitch?' a woman's voice said.

'Speaking.'

'Oh. Hi. Um, it's Veronica. Bing,' she added a beat later.

He lowered his watch arm and wondered how he could have been so preoccupied not to have recognised that voice saying his name in an instant.

Especially when she was the root of his current bout of self-flagellation. The fact that the night before even the memory of Claire hadn't been enough to stop him from trying to make love to her. The mixture of remorse and frustration had turned him completely feral.

'What can I do for you, Ms Bing?' he asked, keeping his voice ultra-professional as he settled back into his chair, which sank to take his weight.

'I was looking for Kristin, actually.'

'So then why did you call my office number?'

'Because I've called your office number a hundred times before and you've never answered. Kristin has. Or she has called me back when I left a message for you. Not that I mind that you answered this time, of course. Just that those past times, when I was actually hoping to speak to you, about Hanover House of course, I got the feeling you were avoiding me. Well, not me, *per se*, just business that you thought beneath you. Or not beneath you so much, but not high on your list of priorities.'

He kept his mouth shut for a few moments before asking, 'Are you finished?'

She laughed softly, and he wondered where she was. Holed up in Boris's office? Leaning on the large reception desk with one leg kicked out behind her? In her crazy pink car?

He glanced at his watch again, instinctively wondering if he had time to pop over and check up close and personal. A moment later he used the hand of that same arm to rub his eyes as he mentally shot the idea down in flames.

'Um, so is Kristin there?'

'She has Thursday afternoons off,' he barked, sitting upright and slamming his feet against the floor so that his toes crunched painfully in his shoe.

'I know. I was just hoping I might catch her before she headed off to get her manicure.' After a pause she added, 'To check if she was up for lunch. It's been a while since I've lived here and I thought she might have an idea of a cool place to catch a bite on a sunny afternoon. But she's not there.'

'She's not here.'

'Right. Then maybe, perhaps, I mean, while I have you here, you could suggest somewhere.'

It occurred to him, belatedly, that perhaps she hadn't called looking for Kristin after all. Had she been looking for an excuse to talk to him? There was her parting comment the night before to consider. She wanted to be friends. Anything else he was reading into the conversation was his own damn fault.

Nevertheless he checked his watch again. But there was no way. He was beyond busy. Work was piling in at a rate of knots. And going to her would have been encouraging something she had been right to call to a halt.

He tucked his phone beneath his chin so that he could tug the damn watch off and throw it across the desk.

'I'd be happy to have my receptionist put together a list of fine choices, which she can e-mail to you at the gallery if that would help.' He closed his eyes and waited for what would no doubt be a scathing response.

'Best not,' she said, her voice a good degree cooler. Pity it didn't translate to the hand holding the phone, which felt as warm as if her hand were in his. 'You're obviously super busy. Meaning, so must your receptionist be. I'll try Kristin's mobile number.'

'Fine.'

'Fine. So I'll leave you to it. Whatever it may be.'

'I'm elbow-deep in contracts. I'm in the process of taking over a medium-sized, Manhattan-based computer-software company.'

'Sounds just the kind of thing worth missing lunch for.'

Mitch ran a finger over his lips, which he was surprised to find were suddenly smiling. No matter how hard she had tried to be cool, she hadn't been able to stop herself from giving herself away entirely.

She might not have called him looking for a lunch date, but she wouldn't have turned him down if he'd offered to join her even after their near miss the night before. Fearless to the ends of her fingers.

'I'll order in a bagel,' he said.

'Promise me you'll not skimp on the red meat to make way for silly things like salad, okay?'

He laughed, despite the tension coursing through the phone line. 'I promise.'

'Good. Well, I guess I'd better go before the boss finds out I'm chatting to you on the company dime. Oh, wait, you are the boss.'

'So you keep reminding me.'

'Mmm. Good luck with your big buyout.'

'Have a nice lunch.'

A stillness settled over the conversation, as though neither of them was quite ready to let go. After she'd had to be the one to do so the night before, Mitch felt the gentlemanly thing to do was take his turn.

'See you at the auction on Saturday, Ms Bing.'

'Not if I see you first,' she said, and then the line went dead, leaving him with a soft buzzing in his ear that sounded a heck of a lot like disappointment.

He lifted the phone away from his ear and stared at the earpiece. 'I'm with you buddy,' he said. 'Life is just that little bit more fun when she's around.'

After he hung up the phone Mitch opened the top drawer of his desk. Beneath a pile of stationery supplies he found what he was looking for. A photograph. Claire sitting among the daffodils in Chelsea's Ranelagh Gardens in London. Smiling serenely. Not a clue she had less than a month to live.

He'd taken the photograph on a rare day that the two of them hadn't been busy with work or research. They'd trawled the King's Road, eaten cheap pizza, and he'd bought her a pink tartan trilby cap that clashed terribly with her auburn hair. They'd both been so busy days like that had been few and far between, but only because they'd thought they had a thousand more such days ahead.

He ran a finger over her cheek, mentally brushing back her fringe. But, where he usually imagined her smile growing as he did so, this day, this time, it was clear he was communing with a photograph and nothing more.

He waited for the resultant pain of that realisation to hit like a sword through the chest.

But it never came.

Veronica held a hand to her face to shield her eyes from the sun as she and Kristin found a shady table outside Greasy Joe's café down the road from her St Kilda apartment.

She sat, put her sunglasses atop her head and shuffled the white plastic chair deeper under the large umbrella's protection.

'Now what have you done to Mitch?' Kristin asked, before she'd even stopped shuffling.

'What's that supposed to mean?'

'This morning the whistling stopped. And I'd left room in my belly for something nice for morning tea and it never arrived.'

Veronica squinted across the table and out to the footpath where a stream of steady pedestrian traffic sauntered past. 'Am I meant to have one single clue why?'

'Come on, Veronica. This is me you're talking to. The girl who pierced your ear in the uni loos. The one who called the ambulance when you passed out. The one who never told another soul that you passed out again the second you saw the drip needle they wanted to put into your arm.'

'That was generous of you,' Veronica said, biting back a grin as she remembered that day, and a hundred like it, that had made her eight months of university the best time of her life. A big, bright, wide-open future ahead of her.

She waited while the waiter placed their matching lemon, lime and bitters on the table and left before saying, 'One thing I can say is that I am loving this job to pieces.'

Kristin shuffled forward, her dark bob swinging from the effort. 'You love it? Really?'

Veronica held on to her drink with both hands until the ice-cold condensation began to sting. 'This morning the Hanover House gang bought me flowers. A hu-u-uge array of pristine white gardenias as someone must have paid attention when I mentioned them in passing at the Friday-night drinks. Isn't that darling? Like they haven't all been working their backsides off this week too.'

'I'm afraid they have a lot riding on your shoulders, my friend,' Kristin said, her mouth quirking nervously.

'I know. And for the first time in as long as I can remember it doesn't faze me. I had begun to wonder if I was cut out for this business. If my need to move on all the time had more to do with a fear of failure than anything else. But I love pulling my Corvette into the car park at work even more than I enjoy driving it there. It really feels as if, if given the chance, I could make Hanover House something really unique and special.'

'So don't wait to be given the chance. Take it.'

'Ah-h-h, but don't you see? That all comes down to Mitch.'

Kristin slumped over her glass, as well. 'Right. Mitch who you kissed. Sorry, Mitch who kissed *you*. Mitch who you obviously did something horrendous to last night to turn him into the Uber-Grouch he was this morning.'

Veronica sipped at her drink. 'It might be because he tried to kiss me again, and this time I didn't let it happen.'

Kristin threw her hands in the air. 'What? You couldn't have just taken one for the team? Was it that bad the first time?'

'God, no,' Veronica said, before she could stop herself.

'No-o-o?' Kristin asked, her voice deep with innuendo.

'No.' Veronica slumped so far she worried if the wind changed, she might never sit upright again, so she rolled her shoulders and leant back into her chair, the warm sunshine spilling across her bare arms and neck instantly reviving.

'So how was it?' Kristin asked. 'Give your poor single friend something to get her through her long, lonely nights.'

'Okay. But then you have to shut up about it. Because it can't happen again.'

Kristin nodded vigorously until her sharp bob messed up enough she looked more like the bright-eyed crazy girl from university.

Veronica unconsciously ran a finger over her bottom lip, re-membering the way Mitch had done the same to her the night before. She imagined the intensity in his quicksilver eyes the moment she'd realised he'd been about to kiss her outside her apartment, and found herself comparing it with the absolute calm she'd seen in him the night before when she'd known he wanted to do so again.

But this conversation was about *the* kiss. Not the almost kiss that would have sealed a deal far more compelling and far more nerve-racking than any deal over some job.

She held her drink to her mouth, needing a kind of shield between her true feelings and her clever friend, then said, 'It was like…magic.'

'Oh, come on. That's movie talk. I want real-life details. Spit level. Is he all teeth? Does he have roving hands? Or how about his tongue—?'

Veronica slapped a hand over her friend's mouth while trying to swallow her next gulp of drink before she sprayed the whole lot over the white plastic tabletop. 'Remind me to never confide in you ever again.'

Kristin pulled back and grinned. 'You're hopeless.'

She was, wasn't she? Stick a cute guy in her way, someone who had an air of 'the provider' and 'the protector' about him, and instead of edging past and averting her eyes she would crash into him. Crash and burn.

Well, not this time. This time felt like her last chance to get a toehold on life. At twenty-six, with a dozen jobs in half as many years under her belt, this truly felt like the time to stop trying so hard to catch up to her peers and make something of the opportunities her life had given her.

She closed her eyes for a moment and repeated the mantra she'd almost forgotten over the past ten days: *Be good. Work hard. Take care of you. Eat more greens.*

She opened her eyes and picked up the menu, determined to start by ordering a green salad. With maybe a side dish of steak and fries because she had such a busy few days ahead of her and would need her strength.

'Veronica and Mitch sitting in a tree—' Kristin sing-songed beneath her breath.

Veronica shot her a flat stare. 'If we were sitting in a tree he'd be lying back on the largest branch neck-deep in his laptop while I'd be hanging on for fear of falling to my death.'

'Still afraid of heights?'

'Oh, yeah,' she said with a shiver.

Kristin grinned. 'And flying? And apricots? And mangoes?'

'I'm not afraid of apricots or mangoes, though they are on a mission to kill me.'

As to tall, dark, handsome men who saw her as the answer to all their connubial dreams? That was one allergy she was yet to completely cut out of her life. But she'd get there. She was sure of it.

'So that's really it? There's no convincing you? You're leaving me with the Uber-Grouch with the zygote blonde fetish for good?'

Veronica nodded. 'I can't go there with someone I work with. I've been there. More than once just after Mum…you know. Stupid, huh?'

'Not stupid. Human. Female.'

'Yeah? Maybe. But this female is all bossed out. From this day forth, I'm all about the job. The work. Look out world, Veronica Bing, clear-headed, single-minded career woman is on the warpath and nothing's gonna get in her way!'

That Saturday night, ten minutes before the auction was due to begin, the feeling in the gallery was electric.

Even hidden away in Boris's office, in which the darling man had set up a small corner desk just for her, Veronica could feel the vibe skittering over her skin like a live current.

She'd never felt more nervous before an auction. Even her first, which had been in the ballroom of a five-star hotel. She shook out her hands, took deep slow breaths and counted backwards from twenty.

Since that first time, auctioneering had felt like so much of her life, something that had happened *to* her rather than something she'd made happen. But here, in this place, on this night as she peeked out the slightly ajar door at the crowd who'd had standing room only since a good hour before start time, she felt *invested*.

She peeked through the door again to seek out several familiar faces in the crowd. Paula Jenkinson, opinionated society doyenne—who as it turned out had thought Veronica fabulous—was there with her husband. As was Bernie Walden, billionaire sporting-goods manufacturer, and Charles Grosse, whom she'd lunched with over the past week upon learning he was, in fact, the premier intermediary agent in town.

'Excellent,' she whispered. They'd come in handy later on.

She scanned the crowd for another familiar face, but was met with a sea of black clothes and shiny hair and glittering jewels and exceptional facelifts. But no tall, dark, handsome Hanover male caught her eye.

She half hoped he might not show. That she could simply do the best job she knew how without continually seeking Mitch out like a ship in stormy weather keeping a close eye on a lighthouse.

Because she hadn't been exaggerating when she'd told Kristin at lunch that her future did come down to Mitch Hanover. If she could keep a tight rein on her wavering self-control, if she could get enough time under her belt to do a great job and to get over the guy, maybe she and her Corvette, and her funky apartment, and her home town stood a chance at creating some kind of permanence for the first time in her adult life.

Suddenly the door pushed open and Veronica stumbled backwards, catching herself on the edge of a grandfather clock.

'Oh, are you okay?' Kristin asked, grabbing her by the shoulder and righting her.

'I'm just fine,' she said, her voice hoarse. She cleared her throat, hoped her unbelievable nerves wouldn't take her voice away completely.

'Are you sure? You look pale.'

Veronica looked down at her bare tanned legs beneath her knee-length tight black satin pants, then over to Kristin's pasty limbs. 'So what does that make you?'

'A Melbournian through and through.'

'Well, then, perhaps my relative paleness is a sign I'm beginning to really fit in here.'

Kristin grinned. 'Not that you're actually so terrified about heading out to the shark pit that you're about to pass out.'

The shark pit. If only that was what had her so anxious. If only it didn't have so much to do with the pressure she had put on herself to be perfect. To do right by the people around her who had already started to feel like the family she'd been without for so long.

And if only she didn't also desperately want to prove to her boss that he should extend her contract beyond six months, despite the raging sexual tension making the whole thing difficult.

The noise outside hushed. The grandfather clock suddenly chimed the hour and Veronica jumped in fright, as did Kristin, who let out a rather loud expletive before clamping her hand over her mouth.

'I'm sure only the first three rows heard you,' Veronica said.

'So long as they all think it was you,' Kristin said, before leaning in for a quick kiss on the cheek, a double thumbs-up, then scurrying out into the gallery proper.

Veronica snuck out after her.

She spied Miriam seated on the other side of the room, and Gerald was there too. The Hanover House staff were scattered throughout the room, holding piles of catalogues, and ready to assist her with pinning down bidders.

The stage was set. The players prepared. Veronica could

kind of feel her toes inside her high black heels if she wiggled them hard enough.

Just as the house lights began to dim, and the Duran Duran CD she had insisted on playing faded into something bland and instrumental, she closed her eyes for a moment, took a deep breath, opened her eyes, and she looked up to see Mitch Hanover in one of his array of nice suits walking towards her looking calm, cool, collected and more gorgeous than any man had the right to be.

She repeated Kristin's earlier oath out loud, but with a much more ladylike volume.

Mitch slowed when he saw Veronica leaning against the door to Boris's office.

Her hair had been blow-dried straight and hung soft and sleek and long from a centre parting. Her eyes were rimmed in lashings of mascara. Her lips were a luscious streak of nude lip gloss. As to the rest of her…

He'd noticed before that she was tall. He'd noticed before that she was nicely put together. But standing there, splashed against the glossy white door, decked out in killer black heels, tight cropped black pants and a matching jacket cinched in at the waist as it hugged her curves and dived into a deep V at her chest, with no evidence of anything beneath, he noticed that the woman was absolutely edible.

'Hey, old buddy, old friend,' she said.

'Tell me you're not wearing that,' was his boorish response.

She cocked an eyebrow. 'I am in fact wearing it. If I was not, I could be arrested for public indecency.'

Mitch thought she could still be arrested for public indecency as it was. In fact, he was finding it physically painful to avert his gaze from her cleavage.

'But it's freezing in here,' he said, even though he knew as a cover it had come far too late.

She unpeeled herself from the door and slowly ambled over to his side. She leant sideways and whispered, 'Can I let you in on a little secret?'

'If you feel you must.'

'I'm deadly nervous right now.'

He glanced at her, keeping his gaze only on things above the neck. 'You? Nervous?'

'Like a deer in hunting season who has just heard a twig crack. I did have a collared shirt on beneath this jacket but it made me feel so hot I thought I was going to pass out. So I just tore the damn thing off.' She glanced up at him from beneath her glorious lashes. 'How's that for fearless?'

Fearless? Who gave a rat's foot about fearlessness right now when the woman beside him had been disrobing behind that innocent-looking white door only moments earlier?

He cleared his throat and dragged his gaze away from her to look out unseeingly into the crowd. 'Are you prepared? Are there any last-minute items you'd like to go over with my mother, or Boris, or, ah, the mousy girl who always runs and hides when I come in? I'm sure she knows a bit about this kind of thing—'

Veronica hit him on the arm so hard he reached up to rub away the pain.

'What was that for?'

'Her name is Gretel. She has a Master's degree in art history. She never says no to working an extra shift. And she runs and hides because she has a crush on you, you big dope.'

Mitch thought coming face to face with Veronica's *décolletage* had him gobsmacked, but the woman seemed to have no limit as to how much she could surprise him. 'Gretel has a crush?'

Veronica's eyes were wide and incredulous as she nodded. Then they narrowed to slits so fast he almost backed up a step in dread. 'Do you have a problem with that? Not blonde enough for you?'

'Don't be ridiculous. She seems perfectly...nice.' He reached up and fixed the knot of his tie, which was feeling rather tight. Perhaps Veronica wasn't nervous, maybe it really was just too hot in here.

When he looked into her eyes again he saw that she was laughing. At him. He let his hand drop. 'You're making fun of me.'

'As much as I possibly can while getting away with it.'

As though she'd heard her name being spoken by him Gretel appeared from nowhere, for once dressed as glossy and slick as Veronica herself. He couldn't help but smile, which produced a little squeak from her direction.

She stood on tiptoe to whisper in Veronica's ear. Veronica listened earnestly, nodded vigorously and grinned at him from the corner of her luscious mouth.

So this was what a *platonic* relationship with Veronica might be like. Fun, teasing, light. And even harder on his hormones than the possibility of more had been.

Lightness he could probably do with. Fun? That would just be an added bonus. And the teasing... Well, the fact that it made him want to grab her by the hand and drag her back inside Boris's old office kind of made the platonic thing a non-starter.

She'd admitted at his parents' house that she was as aware of the simmering attraction between them as he was. Aware and interested. But she'd also been the one to be strong enough to admit that following through would be self-destructive.

And she was right.

She was no carefree young blonde in disguise and he was not on the lookout for anything anywhere near permanent. The very thought made his hair feel hot. He reached up and ran a hand across his forehead to find it was damp with perspiration.

He was torn. Right down the middle. Between what was no doubt an old-fashioned need to honour the memory of his wife, but one he'd clung to for so long he wasn't sure he knew how to let it go, and wanting to allow this once-in-a-lifetime creature to get far, far deeper beneath his skin.

Gretel gave him a brief smile that was more memorable for the colour of her cheeks than anything else, then practically ran away. Soon after the discreet mood music slowly turned off and the crowd noise lowered to an expectant hum.

Mitch slid his hands into his trouser pockets, planted his feet firmly on the floor and looked back at Veronica. 'Gretel, was it?'

Veronica nodded, her eyes twinkling.

'And she has a crush on me?'

'I'm sure she's not the only one. Remember—you do wear very nice suits.'

As seemed to happen more when she was around than any other time, his mouth twitched up into a half-smile. Then he leant in, and whispered, 'Well, the next time you're talking to her about me, let her know I'm evolving.'

'Evolving?'

'Mmm. I've recently found my tastes have begun to run towards sassy brunettes.'

And with that he walked away, not needing to see her exact reaction to know it would be priceless.

He meandered through the crowd, gave his mum a quick 'good luck' kiss on the cheek, patted his father on the shoulder, then took up position standing against the wall beside them.

'Isn't this too exciting?' Miriam asked.

Mitch crossed his arms. 'You've been to a hundred of these things. Surely they all feel the same by now.'

Miriam shuffled forward to sit on the edge of her seat, her eyes now glued to the podium. 'You'd think that, wouldn't you? Nevertheless, here we are tonight, feeling as giddy as schoolkids at our first dance. And I wonder why.'

Mitch followed his mother's eyes to see Veronica striding up to the microphone, her tight pants glimmering in the discreet golden light.

When she hit her mark behind the podium and looked out into the crowd, pinning him for the briefest moment with her gleaming brown eyes, he felt a tightening of his lungs, a racing of his heart and a rush of blood from his extremities to his very centre.

His mother was right. This felt different. This time, for the first time, he felt he had a vested interest in the outcome of the night. And not because he needed the commission, or because he'd somehow seen the light and understood what his parents loved about antiques, but because he wanted Veronica to wow the crowd to the bottoms of their soles.

'Rightio,' Veronica said, her voice booming confidently over the loud speakers. 'You all know where you are, and you all know why you're here. To buy stuff. So let's get down to business. Our first lot of the evening is the sentimental favourite. A piece from the Hanover family collection.'

She nodded into the wings. Gretel came walking out, her cheeks beetroot-red. She carried a hot-pink velvet cushion, adorned with two-inch gold tassels atop which sat Mitch's great-grandmother's engagement ring.

Veronica nodded at Smithy, the Hanover House cleaner who'd spruced himself up for the night and was in charge of the PowerPoint presentation, which would be displaying each lot on the three new LCD TVs scattered in prominent positions around the gallery so that everyone might see.

Mitch felt his mother trying not to look at him. He felt her decade-old disappointment that he'd eloped with Claire after buying her a huge and *new* Tiffany's solitaire as keenly as though she were begging him to stop her from selling the thing. But he kept his eyes dead ahead.

Veronica's voice sang out, 'This piece, a diamond solitaire on a white-gold, diamond-encrusted band once belonged to Amelia Hanover, the wife of the austere-looking gentleman you may have noticed lording it over the reception desk when you first walked in. And, no, I don't mean our very own master curator, Boris Fleming. I mean, the man in the portrait. Phineas Hanover. The gent who started this business a hundred odd years ago.'

The portrait of Phineas scrolled onto the TV screen. Veronica glanced up at it. 'Handsome old goat, don't you think, girls? Especially if you like a moustache on a man as much as I do.'

Laughter drew all the eyes in the room to Paula Jenkinson, who was digging an elbow in her moustachioed husband's ribs.

'Now, Bernie Walden?' Veronica called out, her hand shielding her eyes from the lights. 'I owe you a dollar since your footy team won last night, so how about you start the bidding at a thousand, and I'll add my buck on top?'

'You're a hard woman to say no to,' Bernie called back, raising his finger to make the opening bid of the night. 'A thousand and one dollars.'

The room erupted into laughter. Into frantic bidding. And the energy level in the place threatened to send the roof into outer space. Mitch just shook his head in wonder.

He'd spent the past three years feeling as if he were on some natural mood-leveller. In all that time he hadn't found anything more than mild interest in any of the women who'd flitted in and out of his life.

To make up for it he'd taken bigger business risks just so that he could feel something, anything beyond a dull ache. The past months even the dull ache had begun to fade, leaving him feeling nothing.

And then along came Veronica.

The rush of untempered emotion he now felt reaching out towards his cheeky brunette employee seemed to have opened the release valve for every other emotion kept locked tight inside him for all this time, as well.

He suddenly felt the most debilitating wave of guilt. Guilt that he'd not been more present for Claire, that his work had kept him from her more days and nights than not. Guilt that since returning home, he'd cut himself off from those in his life who still cared enough to put up with him. Guilt that it felt so easy to give this stranger the best of him where others he'd known far longer were missing out.

Mitch didn't wait another second before taking himself, his hormones and his spinning emotions for a walk outside where he could get some much-needed fresh air and a little perspective.

He only wondered if he'd left it too late.

CHAPTER EIGHT

IT WAS near midnight that same night when Veronica walked down High Street, hips swinging, hair bouncing, feeling on top of the world.

Was it only a couple of weeks earlier that she'd been questioning if she was really ready, really experienced enough to step out of small-time auctioneering and into a real-life, big-time, grown-up role?

Ha! She was a genius. A goddess. The best auctioneer on the face of the earth.

As she swung down the back alley her feet felt as if they weren't even touching the ground. She did a little twirl, feet crossing, arms in the air, dancing to some unknown tune in her head, then whipped her car keys from her purse as she spotted her shiny pink car.

In her tight pants she decided not to leap over the door for fear she'd injure herself. Though in all likelihood after the night she'd had she'd feel no pain.

'Need a lift?'

Veronica swore loudly and spun around to find Mitch walking slowly towards her from the other direction. 'You really shouldn't do that. What if I had a stun gun, or nunchakus?'

'I'm not sure quite where you'd hide them in that outfit.'

Veronica looked down. 'You make a fair point. And did you just ask me if I wanted a lift?'

'I did.' He moved out of the shadows to stand beside her. And her car. Which it was unlikely he'd missed. Even though his luminous grey eyes were so fully riveted to her it made her feel even more light-headed than she'd been ten seconds earlier.

She frowned, turned to her car, her keys tinkling in her hand. 'But…'

'Veronica,' he said.

At the hot liquid tone of his voice she turned back to him, car instantly forgotten. 'Yes, Mitch.'

'I'm not ready for tonight to be over.'

Veronica laughed and let her head fall back, feeling almost as though she were filled to the neck with the pink champagne that had flowed all night even though she hadn't touched a drop. 'I know just what you mean! It's some kind of high, isn't it? All those figures flying about the room like everyone in the room had their own mint.'

His eyes were intense when he said, 'I can't imagine getting to sleep for hours.'

'I've had two, maybe three shows like that in my whole career. Don't count on getting to sleep at all.'

She smiled into his eyes, too drunk on success to hide how happy she was to be in that city, on that night, within touching distance of this man.

He stared at her some more before he began pacing from one end of her car to the other, his eyes roving over the clean sleek lines of the Corvette as though he was committing them to memory.

She was about to ask if perhaps he was angling for a lift himself when he said, 'You, Ms Bing, were amazing.'

She felt tight places inside her unfurl at his words. 'You think?'

'I do. And while I'm on the subject I don't just mean tonight.'

'You don't?' In danger of sounding like a parrot, Veronica shook her head and laughed some more. 'It's the profits talking. I've seen *that* before too. New blood brings in new interest. I've been thought of as a rainmaker before and it seems to make guys like you pant.'

The moment the words left her mouth she knew she'd not chosen them wisely. Especially when he stopped pacing and stood directly in front of her, close enough she could see the interest in his eyes had nothing to do with her car. Nothing to do with business, or friendship.

'I don't often pant, Ms Bing.'

'Of course you don't, Mr Hanover. It was daft of me to even suggest it. You're a regular rock.'

He watched her silently for a few brief moments before saying, 'As it turns out, Ms Bing, I'm not so much the rock I thought I was.'

Then, before she knew what was coming, Mitch's arm snuck around her waist and he pulled her up against him and twirled her around until his back was to her car and she had no choice but to grab on to the lapels of his suit.

Her breath whooshed out of her with a lusty, 'Whoa.'

Okay, she thought, *this is just his way of revelling in all the excitement*. She got it. She really did. After big nights where big people dropped huge sums of money, she herself had hugged members of the opposite sex who'd then gone on to get the wrong idea. The tables had simply turned.

But even with that background knowledge, leaning bodily against Mitch, far more intimately than she'd been with him even during their moonlight kiss, her knees went all melty and shaky and every bit of her that touched every bit of him began to purr.

And when his scorching gaze travelled slowly down her face to land upon her lips, she bit the bottom one to stop from moaning with anticipation.

'Mitch,' she said, her voice give-away husky. She wrapped another hand over his arm to keep herself from leaning so fully against him.

'Yes, Veronica.'

'I think you ought to take a mental step back and count to ten before you do anything you might later regret.'

His eyes slid back to hers and she wished she had let him kiss her and be done with it. For the look in his eyes was so fuelled by unquenched desire she thought she might just faint.

She shook her hair from her shoulders and tried to appear far cooler than she felt. 'You and I are not going to do this, remember?'

Mitch licked his lips, and the hand still clutching at his suit grabbed on so tight she feared she might have torn the fabric.

'Tell me why again.'

'Because you're nowhere near ready for the likes of me.'

'That's up to me to decide.'

'Okay. Then because I have no intention of getting horizontal with someone I work with.'

'Then you're fired.'

Veronica snapped to attention quicker than if she'd been doused in a bucket of ice water. 'Hey! You can't—'

'I was kidding. You are the best thing that has ever happened to this business. Though if firing you will get you to stop talking and let me kiss you…'

He moved in, every ounce of him gearing up to do just that. Her heart thumpety-thumped, pitter-patted and tumbled better than a circus clown.

But she managed to track down the last two, maybe three,

wits left with which to lean away and blurt, 'Then we can't because my best friend works for you and there is no way I would jeopardise that. Because there have been far too many blondes in your life for my liking. And because Gretel has a crush on you and us doing this would kill her. And because I don't even like you all that much.'

Okay, so her reasons were a stretch and not even all that close to the actual truth. She would have crossed her fingers if they weren't already heavily involved in hanging on to Mitch.

His beautiful mouth slowly, slowly curved into a lazy, confident smile. He *knew* she was marking time, nothing more. He *knew* she was as ready to go the next step with him as he seemed to think himself ready to do with her. Her throat tightened in a mix of trepidation and exhilaration.

'Mitch, please…'

His finger lifted to rest gently against her lips. 'You work a half an hour drive away in a business I own but have relatively little to do with. Kristin is indispensable and I would never fire someone without cause. And she likes the both of us so I can't see a reason for her to object. As to the blondes, right now, for the life of me, I can't remember a one of them.'

As he spoke his arm slid ever further around her waist until her knee was caught between both of his, until her breasts were squashed against his chest and she had to slide her hand up over his shoulder lest it get crushed. And she quickly discovered then just how rock-like he actually was.

His smile only grew. 'And you do like me.'

'That's a tad arrogant.'

'Have you no idea that your big beautiful brown eyes are like windows with the curtains drawn back? I frustrate you. I annoy you. I confuse you. I intrigue you. And you *do* like me. You like me and you want this. Almost as much as I do.'

Well, if that wasn't just about the nicest half-baked declaration of a man's romantic intentions she'd ever received she didn't know what was.

And she couldn't deny it was more than enough for her suppressed feelings for her boss to spill over from fantasy to real life.

She wanted him so much, and was in no doubt that he wanted her. Maybe giving in to the look in his eye on this magic night would be enough to satiate her feelings for him. Maybe that was all she needed, some physical release, then she could get over him and get on with the job. Maybe he was in the exact same position too. Maybe a herd of flying pigs would come into the gallery next week and ask to put on a show.

Before she figured out which of the above was likely, Mitch used her hesitation to his own advantage and kissed her. And, unlike the gentle exploration of their first kiss, this one was brimming with unchecked passion. He plundered her mouth with his tongue, forcing her into something deeper and stronger than she'd been prepared for.

But instinct kicked in before apprehension took hold.

Her hand on his shoulder dived beneath his hair, tucking beneath the thick strands. Her hand on his arm snuck beneath his jacket until it slid along his torso, pained that it wasn't closer to his hot male skin. Her free leg ran up the outside of his, clamping him to her as he wrapped her tighter still.

His kiss was so potent she had no choice but to simply let everything go: every bad relationship, every bad choice, every bad experience, for they had surely led her to this point. To this place. To this man.

It was so overwhelming she found herself trembling in his arms. He surely felt it too as he only wrapped her tighter, only kissed her more deeply, only did everything in his power to assuage any thoughts that could possibly take away from her pleasure.

Minutes later they pulled apart, the kiss slowing, lengthening, drawing itself out until their lips rested far enough to not be touching, close enough to be breathing in one another's breaths.

'Whoa,' she said again.

Mitch rested his forehead against hers and she felt him smile. 'So do you need a lift?'

And though it was now pretty obvious he hadn't come looking for her for just a friendly congratulatory kiss, and that they had crossed a line she'd sworn she never would, Veronica said, 'I thought you'd never ask.'

Much later that night, Mitch sat on the back veranda of his far-too-big-for-one-person Richmond Hill pad wearing nothing more than soft grey flannel boxer shorts and a frown.

With his bare toes curled around the cold wrought iron railing, he stared out over the green trees and tiled roofs of the lush eastern suburbs of Melbourne, which were bathed in swathes of silvery moonlight.

The soft whoosh of traffic below soothed him as it always did on the many nights he'd found himself in this exact position long after the witching hour had claimed most of the city to sleep.

Though in the past he'd been alone out there with his thoughts, on this night he had a small velvet box in his hand. He lifted it to eye-level and twirled it back and forth. It weighed no more than a fifty-cent piece, but the treasure inside it had cost him far more.

The lanky kid he'd asked to bid on it for him at the auction had obviously thought him off his nut when he'd told him he'd go as high as the auctioneer would take him. But when he'd slipped the kid a fifty, he'd gone about the business of bidding with such ease Mitch had struggled against putting a halt to his endeavour from the other side of the room.

In the end he'd paid a song for the thing, almost double its listed value. But he could afford it. Even if he wasn't quite sure what he was going to do with it.

Give it to his mother? Donate it to the gallery as a show-piece to match the portrait of Phineas Hanover? Or save it for a rainy day?

At that last thought he waited for his distracted heart to twist, for the image of a beautiful, doe-eyed, auburn-haired angel to swim before his eyes.

When this time she didn't even appear in his mind's eye the very moment he conjured her, he softly called out her name.

'Claire Bear,' he said, his voice croaky. But again she chose to stay away.

Though this time, for the first time in three years, her absence brought about a measure of peace.

He breathed in the cool spring air, the tang of the lemon tree taking up the far left-hand corner of his large balcony stinging the back of his throat. At least that was what he told himself the sensation was.

A few quiet moments later he tossed the velvet box high in the air, caught it and headed inside where a beautiful, willing, vital brunette auctioneer lay naked in his bed.

Veronica awoke to an eyeful of sunshine pouring through ceiling-to-floor gauzy white drapes flapping softly against a pale green-papered wall. She rubbed her eyes and rolled over to feel the slippery, high-thread-count, cotton sheets sliding over bare skin.

Yep. Bare. Naked. No camisole and three-quarter-length pyjama bottoms, as she usually wore. She pulled the sheets to her neck as she waited for her sleepy brain to catch up to her other senses.

'Good morning.'

She turned her head so fast she almost got whiplash, to find Mitch walking into the room.

Okay. Right. Of course. She was smack bang in the middle of the morning after sleeping with her boss.

She wanted to slap herself across the forehead, but that would have meant letting go of the sheet and allowing Mitch an eyeful of...everything he'd already seen, if her fast-returning memories were correct.

His knee-length charcoal Paisley cotton robe flapped open as he walked, revealing soft grey cotton boxers and a whole lot of tanned, muscled, manly skin. His feet were bare. His hair was ever so slightly mussed. And her mouth began to water.

Sexy, sexy, sexy, slid through her mind, bringing with it wave after wave of renewed desire. *Bad, bad Veronica. Act cool. Be pleasant. And get the hell out of here before you make things any worse.*

She made to sit up and bring the sheet with her when she realised he was carrying a tray loaded with orange juice, a plate of thick white toast dripping in melted butter and plum jam and a single native flower in an old jam jar.

Breakfast in bed? She'd never had a man make her breakfast in bed. In fact, she'd never had anyone make her breakfast in bed. She'd done it herself that many times for her mum she couldn't remember one from another. But this... Mitch... Doing so off his own bat...

The pitter-patter thumpety-thumps didn't take long to return and thus she found herself, rather than making excuses and leaving, slowly, slowly propping an arm on the pillow and leaning her head on her upturned palm.

'Has your gown been ironed?' she asked as she grabbed and bit into a corner of jam-covered toast as he passed.

He glanced down. 'By the looks of it.'

'You didn't do it yourself?'

His gaze slid back to her, one eyebrow raised. 'I don't exactly have the time. I have a laundry service who do such things for me.'

'So the starched shirts...'

'Out of my hands.'

She nodded, and smiled through her full mouth.

'Is that all right with you?' he asked as he sat on the edge of the bed.

'I'm not sure. I kind of liked the fact that you were so straight.' She reached out and ran her hands through his hair until it sat up in messy spikes. 'But I find I also like that you don't mind getting ruffled.'

He hooked his legs up onto the bed: long, muscular, sprinkled with dark hair. He watched her eat for some while before she realised she was the only one indulging.

She swallowed and asked, 'Are you not having any?'

He shook his head.

'I'm sure your mother would tell you breakfast is the most important meal of the day.'

'I'm sure she would. I usually grab something from the café downstairs from work.'

From Stacy? Veronica wondered, though she bit her tongue. Their night together might well have been the wrong move, but it had been something special. Mitch's aptitude, his tenderness, his generosity in bed were second to none. It had been a night she would never in her whole life forget.

It'd had nothing to do with the Stacys in Mitch's life, before or after her. It had been purely about the two of them, and the feelings they had for one another, no matter how unfortunate they might have been. As she slept alone in her own bed the next night and the next she could hang on to that at least.

Changing the subject, she asked, 'So what exactly do you do in your big city office apart from find brilliant people to work for you and make you look good?'

'We invest in emerging markets.'

She nodded, and acted impressed, as if she knew what that meant.

Mitch nodded along with her. 'You have no idea what I'm talking about, do you?'

'Not a single clue. Do emerging markets have anything to do with...maternity clothes?'

'I'll give you a moment to think about that.'

Veronica looked up at the ceiling and nibbled at her lower lip as she pretended to think really, *really* hard.

'I wouldn't do that,' he said.

His voice rumbled in that rumbling way that Veronica now knew meant it was worth her giving him her full attention. She turned on her side and faced him. 'You wouldn't do what?'

He reached out and traced his thumb across her bottom lip. 'Hasn't someone older and wiser explained that when you nibble on your lip like that it drives men crazy?'

She looked around the room. 'Men? Plural?'

'Fine. This one man. Those lips of yours have kept me up nights.'

'Including last night, if I remember correctly.'

She'd hoped for a laugh, something to ease the intensity in his gaze, but she only got more intensity for her efforts. She put the half-eaten toast back on the tray before her suddenly dry mouth made her choke on it.

He moved the tray from the bed to the bedside table. 'When you walked in through the doors of Hanover House with those lips attached to that face combined with these shoulders…' his hands trailed over every part of her anatomy that he mentioned until he slowly pushed the sheet down her arm, baring her naked skin to the morning light '…and that waist, and those hips, how could I not give you the job?'

She somehow managed to keep her voice from spiralling into soprano range as she said, 'You hired me for my lips? That's a tad presumptuous, don't you think? You couldn't have had one clue you were going to get anywhere near these lips. These lips are—'

'Delicious,' he said.

And yours to do with as you please, she thought at the exact same time that he leant down and claimed them.

She didn't push him away. She couldn't. Didn't want to.

The kiss remained tentative, as though the two of them were keeping a tight hold of the brakes for fear if they let go they'd careen downhill so fast they would spin totally out of control.

But when she leant up to him, wrapping a bare arm around his neck until her naked torso slid against his hairy chest, Mitch groaned. At least she was pretty sure it was Mitch.

He kissed the side of her mouth, the patch of sensitive skin just below her ear, the spot at the base of her neck where her tendons clenched in ecstasy.

It was bliss. And it couldn't last.

Her eyes shot open and she blinked up at the ceiling. 'You've done this before.'

She felt his laughter rumble from his chest to hers, but rather than dampening her runaway feelings the intimacy only made them spiral further out into the big wide world.

'Once or twice,' he said. 'Hope that doesn't scare you away.'

She tilted her head to give him better access. 'I'm fearless, remember.'

Fearless? Ha! Mitch Hanover made her feel as if she were a thousand little tiny pieces of paper held together with nothing stronger than crazy glue. As if he had it in his power to tear her, and her determined independence, apart. And a man in his position wasn't on the lookout for someone with whom to spend a lifetime.

When a rising heat started at her toes and bled quickly to her thighs she knew things were getting to the point that reason was about to fly out the window. She gently moved away, slowly enough so as not to be obvious, and obvious enough that Mitch's lips left her skin and he unwrapped his arms from around her.

'Thanks for breakfast, but it's time I head on home. Plants to feed, clothes to wash, nosy superintendent to shock when I turn up in the same clothes I wore last night.'

She tried carefully rearranging the sheet to give herself a modicum of modesty, but when she ended up tipping Mitch halfway off the bed with one great tug she gave up.

'Allow me,' he insisted, before he took off his robe and wrapped it around her shoulders, helping her arms into the sleeves that smelt like him and carried his warmth.

He closed it over her breasts and tied the sash as he said, 'I want to see you again.'

She tried her darnedest to keep from staring at his beautiful naked torso. 'You know where I work. You can see me every day if you so desire.'

He brushed a strand of hair from her cheek and her eyes rose to his. 'That's not what I mean and you know it.'

And what she saw in his eyes made her heart beat so hard

she was scared it was making cookie-cutter shapes through her skin. He was serious. Deadly serious. So much for last night being a way to assuage the sexual tension that had hampered their working relationship from day one.

Meaning the something special could be repeated. Meaning the bliss didn't have to end. Yet. How could she say no?

'So like what? You want to actually ask me out on a date?'

'Only if I thought you might say yes.'

Yes, yes, YES! her subconscious screamed. But the part of her that had been here and done that and left town with only the T-shirt on her back reminded her to not get ahead of herself. Kristin had made it clear the blondes got three dates. Why should she think herself any different?

'I have one condition,' she said, before she'd even felt the words forming. 'One that is non-negotiable.'

His hand dropped away, his face coming over all haughty and boss-like. It helped. 'And that would be?'

'We keep it to ourselves.'

He didn't even blink. And didn't make a move to negate the idea. So she found herself running with it for all she was worth.

'Business during business hours. Play only after hours. No strings. No promises. No blame game when the time comes that either of us decides to call it quits. I won't have it any other way.'

She wouldn't? She *really* wouldn't? For Mitch Hanover surely she could make an exception… No! Exceptions had toppled her in the past. And this time, with this job, and this guy, she was in danger of screwing everything up royally unless she kept tight rein on every piece of the puzzle that was her fragile life.

She held out a hand. 'So do we have a deal?'

The only give-away sign that Mitch had even heard her was

the gentle up and down movement of his Adam's apple as he swallowed.

Please tell me you are hesitating because you will never agree as you now realise you actually adore me to pieces and want to tell the world how much, her weak heart cried.

Tell me you will never agree to the pact because you now see this was the one and only time for us and we should both move on and enjoy a nice working relationship before anything messy puts a stop to that possibility, her stubborn head begged.

Then his cheek did the twitch thing and Veronica's internal plea of the heart drowned out everything else inside her until she thought she might burst.

And then he said, 'It's a deal,' while shaking her hand with all the romance of a business agreement.

Veronica's heart and head both threw their hands in the air and decided it was just all too hard and they didn't want to play anymore.

CHAPTER NINE

A few days later, Mitch came to from staring out his office window. He swung his chair back around to face his office proper and blinked to find Kristin watching him as she slowly folded her flexible rubber keyboard into its leather pouch with her BlackBerry.

'Sorry, did you say something? I was a million miles away.'

'You've been a million miles away all week. Since the auction, in fact. And I think I know where you've been.'

The confrontational tone of her voice had him deliberately righting his chair. His voice was cool as he asked, 'And where's that?'

'With Veronica.' She clasped her hands together on her lap. 'Tell me nothing's going on between you two, and I won't say another word about it.'

'Why? Have you been talking to her? What did she say?'

Kristin threw her hands in the air. 'Well, there's my answer. You can't do this to her, you know. I won't let you.'

'Do what, exactly?'

She crossed her arms and glared at him. 'What you do. With the blondes. I'm not buying goodbye flowers for her, I tell you that right now.'

'Who says you'll need to?'

Kristin's eyebrows disappeared beneath her dark choppy fringe. 'Are you saying you can see yourself dating Veronica for an extended period of time? Moving in with her? Marrying her?'

Her words stung him like arrows shot at close range. But then, as the images they invoked sank in—waking up next to Veronica again and again as he had on Sunday morning, sharing sections of the newspaper over the kitchen table, being able to touch her, and kiss her and laugh with her whenever he pleased—the arrows dissolved and fluttered away.

He wondered, and not for the first time, how long it might take before he'd tire of that sassy smile, those dark brown eyes, that riot of dark curls, the crazy, sexy attire, the generosity of spirit, the veiled vulnerability that nobody else bar him seemed to notice....

'*If* I chose to start seeing Veronica, and I'm not saying I have, I don't think three dates would cut it,' he said, giving Kristin as much insight into his private thoughts as he thought necessary. Or prudent, considering Veronica had asked they keep their assignation quiet.

'Right,' Kristin said, frowning, not as appeased as he'd hoped she might be. 'And how about three weeks? Three months. Three years—'

'Stop,' he barked. 'Right now.'

He held up a hand and Kristin's mouth snapped shut.

'None of us can see that far ahead. It's not fair on anybody to even try. Besides, she's told me on a number of occasions that six months is about her limit in any job, so that seems a nice demarcation line for us to aim towards. If we were of a mind to aim for anything,' he added belatedly.

Kristin's mouth hung open for several seconds before she asked, 'Does Veronica know this? That your soft spot for her has a built-in lifespan?'

'Of course. In fact, it was her suggestion.'

Okay. So much for keeping things quiet. Mitch rubbed a hand hard over his mouth and silently cursed himself. And Kristin and her incessant needling.

Kristin merely scoffed. 'And you believed her?'

'Are you telling me I ought not to have?'

'Hell, no. Not about this.' Her hands were wringing so tight her knuckles turned white. 'The thing about Veronica... She's got this huge heart. Which, if you're anywhere near as smart as I think you are, you've worked out for yourself.'

She glared at him long enough he had to nod to admit he had, in fact, noticed the size of her heart. Though even that confession was enough to have him shifting in his chair as if he'd been picked out of a line-up by the Spanish Inquisition.

'She had to give up on studying business at uni to look after her ailing mum when she was like eighteen.'

'Her mother had Alzheimer's.'

At that Kristin's glare turned to shock, which he'd kind of hoped it would. Serve her right for being so impertinent.

'Right, so she told you that when her mother died, she was left with nothing, no house, no money, as every cent had gone into caring for her mum?'

Mitch's sanctimonious smile faded away. She had not, in fact, told him any of that. She'd left out the fact that, not only was she gorgeous, and vivacious and so full of life she made him feel as though he'd finally been allowed back into the light after three years living in a self-imposed dark room, she was gutsy. Loyal. And truly heroic.

When he opened his mouth this time, Kristin held up a flat palm.

'Then,' she said, with all the gusto of a preacher in the pulpit, 'she worked three jobs to earn enough to get herself on her feet before finding her niche in auctioneering. Yet since the gods had long since decided against making her journey on this earth easy, she has been run out of town on more than one occasion because some guy she worked with didn't see beneath the exterior gorgeousness and innate kindness to realise she was not a woman to toy with.'

He sat back, his earlier smugness swallowed back down into the cavity of his chest. That he did know, for Veronica had tried to tell him so when she'd pushed him away at his parents' house. And then Saturday night he'd had to get all he-man on her and damn the consequences.

'Thank you for telling me. I'll certainly keep all that in mind.'

Her eyes narrowed at his composed words. 'You hurt her and I will kill you.'

'What kind of guy do you think I am? I have no intention of hurting her.'

Kristin tilted her head and looked at him as if he were slow of hearing. But how on earth could he possibly hurt…? Oh…

Moments of his life over the past month tumbled into place until they merged with the precision of a Swiss watch. The way he felt her watching him across a crowded room. The way her eyes said no while her body said yes. And the way she melted beneath his kisses, as if his arms held about her were the only things keeping her from falling at his feet.

He might have been trying very hard to convince himself this could turn out to be one of the more satisfying flings of his lifetime. Even admitting to himself that being with her could be liberating. All the while it seemed that effervescent Veronica Bing might well be out there in the world right now hoping for much more.

Thus finally admonished, he summoned up the face that made his employees quiver in fear. 'Are you quite done?'

Kristin's mouth twitched as though she was about to find more in her arsenal, but she must have realised that in issuing a death threat she'd pushed his patience quite far enough. 'I'm done.'

'Good, because so am I.' He waved a hand in the general direction of his door.

She stood and straightened her suit some as she pursed her lips and slowly edged her way to his office door. She turned with her hand on the frame. 'Mitch, I didn't mean—'

'Yes, you did.'

He got a weak smile before she closed his door with a soft click.

And the moment he was alone he sat against the back of his chair with a thud.

If Kristin was right...what did that leave?

Letting Veronica go before she did him the world of good he knew in his bones she would? Or allowing himself to consider she might actually be the end and not the means?

The choices seemed pretty black and white and for a guy who'd lived in a cloud of grey for so long he wondered if he ever might be able to remember which was which.

It had been days since Veronica had heard from Mitch.

She should have been delighted at the fact. Delirious. She'd met a man who actually *listened* to her concerns about embarking on a Relationship with a capital *R*.

But naturally, being that she was completely perverse, each and every day since a little voice in the back of her head had told her that it might be nice to hear from him. To get a bunch of flowers out of the blue. To be left sneaky little love messages on her mobile.

There was none. She'd checked. Every five minutes.

So on the Wednesday afternoon, when she heard his voice come from the region of Boris's—and her—office doorway saying, 'Howdy, stranger,' she was fairly certain she'd imagined it.

She looked up from her computer where she'd been searching the Internet for local artists in preparation for a show she was hoping to put together a few months down the track to find out her imagination could take the day off.

For there Mitch stood; he and a jet-black suit, a snow-white shirt and a shot-silk, baby-blue tie that did things to his eyes that made her stomach fair flip over on itself.

'Hi, yourself,' she said, her voice as breathy as if she were channelling Marilyn Monroe.

He leant his large form against the doorjamb and slid his hands into his pockets. Veronica did her best to keep her breathing under control.

With a nod towards her computer, he asked, 'What are you doing?'

'Working hard for the man.'

She slid her feet from her high heels and plopped them onto her desk. Mitch's eyes turned dark just as she'd known they would. She was a bad girl. But she was also a girl who desperately did not want him to see how affected she was just to be seeing him in the flesh for the first time since their confusing morning after the most sweet, tender, vulnerable, intimate night before she'd ever experienced.

'Hope he's paying you what you're worth,' Mitch said, his dark voice sliding over her like a river of melted chocolate.

'Not nearly. Why? You think you can make me a better offer?'

He pushed away from the door and sauntered towards her, his eyes gleaming like a cat with its eye on easy prey. 'Wish I could. But my hands are tied. You see I already have this minx of a woman taking up valuable space in just the kind of position I think you would fill perfectly.'

Her heart stopped. Just like that it came to a dead halt. Forgot how to work. Gave up. As she was pretty sure they weren't talking about work anymore.

She coughed and her heart remembered where it was and began beating once more, though with not nearly as much fanfare as before.

As he neared she was reminded of how good he smelled, and that there really wasn't anything she could do to shield herself against all that yumminess. Especially when he sat on the corner of the desk and brought her feet to his lap, where he began to trace circles beneath her toes.

In response she casually edged the spaghetti strap of her ice-blue camisole off her shoulder, leaving it bare. Just because she couldn't stop herself from falling more for the guy every day didn't mean she wouldn't resort to playing dirty.

'And what position is that?' she asked. 'Should I limber up?'

She snuggled her foot deeper into his lap, her toes tickling at the top button of his pants, and he grabbed her toes before she could go any further.

'From what I can see you're limber enough.'

Limber enough? Did what he had in mind suggest it would be wise to lock the door? Or was that code for *Don't push me*? Had their dalliance been a welcome-to-the-company special? Were they part-time lovers? Could they be more? And even if that possibility was something she had found herself envisaging during her weaker moments, could he?

And when and how would it all end? Maybe that was what she really wanted to know: not what they were but for how long. And could they continue to work together after it all came tumbling down like a house of cards?

Veronica's head felt as if it were about to pop. And when he didn't speak, or move or even look as if he had a clue as to the answer of any of the above questions, she slowly dragged her feet away from his blissful touch and gently lowered them back into her shoes and pretended everything was normal.

'So to what do we owe the pleasure of your company? Checking I haven't spent any more of your hard-earned dosh on frippery?'

He remained where he sat, cruelly continuing to envelop her in his signature scent that only served to bring forth the memory of waking in his bed.

'I'm fine with the frippery,' he said. 'I mean, it's not exactly the kind of frippery I'd use in my own home, but it did the job the other night.'

She wondered if she was the kind of frippery he'd keep in his home longer than a night. And then she mentally slapped herself for having such a one-track mind.

Business hours were for business. That was what they'd said. What *she'd* made him promise. And he'd agreed.

She breathed in the office's pervading scent of old wood and dust and silver polish that was becoming just as familiar and far more comforting every day she spent in the place and pointed at the computer monitor. 'Then how about I show you the brilliant lightbulb idea I had? It's kind of been bubbling away since I chatted with a couple of local artists after the auction.'

He hopped up from the desk, wandered around to her side. She slid her strap back atop her shoulder and squashed her bottom into a more comfy spot in her chair. But all fidgeting came to a halt when Mitch's hand slid over her shoulder, tucked a finger beneath the camisole strap and let it fall down her arm again.

When he bent and his mouth traced a row of kisses at the

point where her neck met her shoulder her eyes fluttered closed and she gave up on trying to be blasé.

She turned and quickly found herself in his arms. He dragged her to her feet until she was bodily against him. Her bare skin sliding against the glorious fabric of his suit jacket.

He leant in for a kiss but at the last second she managed to tip her head just out of reach. 'What happened to work hours being out of bounds?'

'Don't dress like that in the workplace and we might stand a chance.'

She let her hand trace around his ear and down the side of his neck until his grey eyes lost all light. 'You can't tell me what to wear or what not to wear, Mitch. It's against the rules of workplace relations.'

When she moved in to place a kiss on the corner of his mouth, this time he was the one to lean away.

'You know a hell of a lot more about workplace-relations laws than any person not working in the field has any right to know.'

She shrugged. 'Let's just say I've had reason to know my rights in the past.'

'And what did you learn?'

'I learnt that a girl has to look after her own interests because, when it comes down to it, it's mighty rare to find anyone else who will.'

She looked up from his tempting mouth and into his eyes, expecting them to be gleaming from the tension of self-denial. But they were not. They were deadly serious.

And finding herself so tightly wrapped within his arms, coiled about him so intimately, while not knowing him nearly well enough to understand what had suddenly made him so grim was enough to shoot a thread of alarm down her spine.

She stopped caressing his neck, and made to unhook her calf from around his.

'Don't,' he said, his voice hoarse.

She stopped what she was doing and clung to him. 'Why?'

'Because I haven't yet managed to kiss you.'

The alarm flipped over on itself and fast became a thrill. 'You've managed for three days without doing so. Who says you can't survive another three? Or longer.'

He slid his arm tightly around her waist and pressed her hard against him. His voice rumbled from his chest directly through hers when he leant so close to her lips she could feel his breath as he said, 'Who says I managed?'

And with that he kissed her.

Three days? The way she dissolved in his arms it felt more as if it had been three months. And she knew she didn't want to go another three months, three days or three hours without this feeling again.

The way he kissed her blocked out every other concern she had about them. About his past, his reluctance to have a future. About her own deeply set need to survive on her own. Because when he kissed her, she didn't feel as if she was merely surviving. She felt worshipped. She felt ravaged. She felt wicked. She felt new.

She felt as if she was finally living.

The kiss came to a natural lull when the laws of human anatomy intervened and they had to pull apart to breathe.

He looked into her eyes. She looked into his. From one to the other. Hoping to discover within the dark grey depths how he felt about her. Or even if he felt one hundredth of the depth of how she felt about him.

For now, in that moment it struck her with undeniable clarity how she felt.

She was in love with him.

Having the realisation wrap itself about her like a silken rope was at once the most liberating, most hellish and least simple moment of her life. One she couldn't hope to accommodate while clinging to him as she was.

'So you don't want to hear my bright idea?' she asked.

He blinked down at her, all gorgeous confusion, until she pointed over her shoulder at the computer.

'I'm afraid I don't have time. E-mail it to me.'

She let go so that she could shoot him a saucy salute. 'Yes, boss.'

He reached up and traced his thumb along her right cheek-bone. 'I'm serious. E-mail it to me. Any ideas, any time. I value your input.'

Okay, so if she thought she loved him before, his utterly faithful declaration of his respect for her only made her want to leap into his arms and ask him where he'd been all her life.

But then she remembered. He'd been married. He'd lost a woman who had truly made him happy. And he'd been purposely dating women he saw no future with.

While she'd been taking care of everyone else in her life, bar herself, to the point that now she found it almost impossible to differentiate esteem for love.

Not this time, she shouted inside her head. *Not. This. Time.*

'Go, then,' she said, pushing him away. 'Go now. And check your e-mail the minute you get back to the office. There'll be a file there waiting for you.'

'I will.' His smile was easy. Far too easy as he backed away.

She followed like a pathetic puppy as he waltzed out of the office, through the gallery and down the stairs into the foyer.

'Hang on,' she said, reaching out and grabbing him by the elbow before he made a clean getaway. 'You never told me why you were here.'

'I thought I told you quite satisfactorily, actually.'

He reached up and placed a finger beneath her chin, then leant in for another kiss. And while their other kisses had been fraught with discovery and immediacy and passion and need, this kiss was no more than a feather-light touch of their lips.

Her eyes wavered closed as she breathed in his scent, as she tasted his unforgettable taste, as the finger resting lightly beneath her chin filled her with his warmth.

As she watched him walk away she lent a finger against her lips, marking his place for whenever he next wanted to continue where he left off.

'Was that Mr Hanover?' Gretel asked, coming from nowhere with an armful of old cushions. Boris followed hot on her heels carrying nothing but his own creaky frame.

Veronica sucked her bottom lip into her mouth hoping to hide any swelling Mitch's kiss might well have imparted. Then she scooted behind the reception desk and pretended she was diligently looking for something very particular while her mind whirled with the hope they hadn't seen her kissing the boss.

'Sure was,' she sing-songed.

'What did he want?' Boris asked.

'Ah, he was just in the neighbourhood so popped in to say hi. So *hi* from Mitch!'

Gretel swooned, while Boris frowned.

'He never checked up before,' he said as he looked out into the gallery with a worried expression on his face.

'It's okay, Boris,' Veronica said. 'Truly. He only had good things to say.'

The fact that they weren't about the gallery was beside the point. She felt her cheeks warm at the lingering memory of the kiss still imprinted upon her, and at her own idiocy in letting things go as far as they had.

'Ah-h-h,' Boris said, his cheeks pinking. 'I see.'

'You see what?' Gretel asked.

Nothing! Veronica screamed internally. *He's a sweet old man. He sees nothing!*

'Nothing,' he said, shaking his head while watching Veronica all too carefully.

She couldn't look him in the eye as she knew he knew and she didn't want to know what he must have thought of her because of it.

It was Geoffrey all over again, but this time the rumours would all be true. Though Boris would be discreet, her other co-employees would figure it out. They'd start talking about her behind her back. They'd lose trust in her, thinking she would side with the boss rather than with them.

And it would get so uncomfortable she'd have to leave.

'Anyhow,' she said, her voice falsely bright, 'I mentioned our little local artist proposal, Boris, and he said he'd love to have a look. I hope you don't mind if I shoot an e-mail over to him while it's fresh in my mind.'

'Not at all.'

'Right. Good. Excellent. Okay. So keep up the good work.'

Before she said anything else that made them look at her as though she'd begun to lose her mind, she spun away and practically jogged up the back stairs.

But, rather than heading for the office, she slipped out the back loading-bay door and didn't stop moving until she was in her car, with the top down, hair flying behind her, flapping hard and fast about her ears.

The wind slapping her face also did a good job of whipping something that felt a heck of a lot like angry tears streaming from her eyes as she realized, not only had she set in motion reasons galore to lose the first job she'd ever felt was truly made for her, but she was also in love with a man who would never be ready to love her back.

CHAPTER TEN

MITCH got in his car and drove. He had no particular destination in mind, all he knew was that he wasn't ready to be anyplace in particular.

He'd gone to Hanover House looking for answers, and boy had he found them.

When Veronica had looked up and seen him… His heart contracted in his chest at the mere memory of the way she had become lit from within and her feelings for him had shone from her eyes for all the world to see.

A red light brought him to a halt somewhere in the region of Prahran. He cricked his neck, rolled his shoulders and closed his eyes, basking in the warm spring sunshine, hoping it might help his thoughts coagulate into something resembling wisdom.

The first truth that settled about his shoulders was that Kristin was right. Veronica had feelings for him.

The second truth was that while months earlier it would have, the knowledge didn't spook him one little bit.

That was because before Veronica he'd felt cold-blooded. Sluggish. Solitary. Impenetrable. He'd needed to be in order to survive his life. His loss.

And since Veronica, his whole world felt turned upside

down. His life had become unpredictable, engrossing. His mind had wandered. His chest had opened itself to laughter. And his heart… The heart he'd promised to Claire on their wedding day. The heart that had turned to ice when he'd lost her. That heart had begun to thaw.

He glanced in the rear-view mirror and caught his own re-flection. He hardly recognised himself. Because the greatest truth was that since Veronica he had stopped merely surviving his life and had begun to live it again.

No wonder her old boss had done whatever he thought he had to to keep her. How gormless would a man have to be to let someone like her walk out of his life? Genius that he was he'd set things up so that in less than six months he'd know exactly how it felt to let her go. Now who was the schmuck?

He looked deep inside himself, searching for Claire. Wanting, needing her permission to move on. Like a mirage far far away he saw her smile. He felt her touch. He knew she'd want him to be happy.

A car horn sounded behind him and he glanced up to find the light was green.

He looked back in the mirror, blew his wife one last kiss and felt a gentle peace come over him as he finally let her go.

Several car horns joined the first and Mitch shoved his foot on the accelerator and his black sports car tore down the road.

He turned down the next available side street, did a scream-ing U-turn, whipped the car from third gear into fourth and into the future. As, before he went in search of the rest of his life, he had to make a quick detour to a drawer in the hall table of his Richmond Hill apartment.

And then he would go out in search of the answer to all his dreams. Now that he knew her name was Veronica Bing.

* * *

Veronica lay back on the creaky old sun lounger on her roof atop her apartment building. She should have thought to have brought a towel if she didn't want to end up with permanent cane marks on the backs of her legs. But thinking hadn't been high on her list of priorities when she'd trudged up there.

A Bloody Mary rested, half drunk, on the concrete next to her. Her eyes were closed to the weak Melbourne spring sunshine. Her skirt was hitched up to her hips, her top tucked into her bra every which way so as not to ruin her fading Gold Coast tan.

And she did her best to clear her mind and come up with a new plan. The *be good, work hard, take care of you, eat more greens* mantra hadn't brought her much in the way of luck.

She'd worked hard. Harder than she'd ever worked in her life. True, she hadn't taken care of herself in the way she'd hoped she might, her care split between her work, her colleagues, her friend, her boss, her boss's family, her clients, her clients' agent…and goodness knew who else she'd put first. Her greens intake over the past weeks had amounted to celery in her Bloody Marys. And, last but not least, by falling in love with her boss she'd been the opposite of good.

Though surely one of out four wasn't bad.

Her mobile phone beeped. She thought about not answering it. There was nobody she wanted to talk to right now. But she was listed as an emergency contact with Hanover House's alarm-system firm, so her diligence got the better of her.

She kept her eyes closed, felt around her thigh until she found it, then opened one eye to read the message.

'Where are you?' it read, and it was from Mitch.

'No how are you?' she said aloud. 'No wish you were here. No I must have you now and for ever but only after I've given you a foot rub and made you dinner. Typical.'

Her thumb paused over the keys and she thought about telling him she was halfway to Adelaide. Instead she turned her phone to silent and slid it back beneath her thigh and shuffled back to a semi-comfortable spot.

'Lucky for you I'm a man who isn't afraid to ask for directions.'

Her eyes flung open and she stared into a darkening sky framed by massive potted palm trees that made do for a rooftop garden.

She turned her head to find Mitch standing at the top of the stairs leading to the roof. She could only hope he hadn't been standing there long.

'I hope I'm not intruding.' His gaze slid slowly down her body until it rested at the top of her bare thighs.

She reached down and tugged until her crushed skirt covered all the bits it was made to cover up. 'How did you find me here?'

'I asked the super. He said he saw you come up here about an hour ago and hadn't seen you come down.'

'The super? That's a tad creepy.'

'And I made sure he knew I thought so too. I don't think he'll be keeping as close an eye on you in the future. Though without his little crush on you I might never have found you, so I can't hate the guy entirely.'

'How nice. Perhaps you can invite him over to watch the footy at your place on the weekend. He seems a beer-and-pizza kind of guy.'

It was about then that Veronica wondered if he was ever going to explain what he was doing there. So she asked, 'What are you doing here, Mitch?'

He took the last two steps up the stairs, his long legs carrying him towards her far too quickly considering she only just remembered the state of her top. She sat up and unhooked as best she could, then did her best to look professional while reclining barefoot on a tacky cane sun lounger.

When she realised he was about to sit on the end of her chair, she tucked her legs up and over the side.

He sat. The chair groaned. She dug her toes into the still-hot concrete and curled her fingers around the edge of the chair.

'I've come to tell you that the deal we made has become unworkable.'

She felt her blood rush from her face, her arms, her torso, her feet. 'But why? You can't! We have a contract. And the auction—'

He smiled at her and she stopped blabbering and waited to let him tell her what he meant before jumping to any more conclusions.

'I don't mean your contract, Veronica. You must know I'm perfectly happy with how you are going about your job. More than happy, in fact. I'm ecstatic, if you must know the truth.'

Her blood came back, pooling in her cheeks, and the backs of her knees. 'It seems I must.'

He nodded, watching her, carefully, his eyes unnaturally dark considering the light still left in the day. 'I mean, the deal we made that morning at my place. After the night you stayed.'

'Oh.' She thought back. The 'I want to see you again so long as business is business' deal. She sat up straight. 'Oh-h-h.'

'Things in my life have recently come to light to show me that I was presumptuous to agree to your terms.'

She nodded, though her skin felt as if it were being torn from her body piece by tiny piece as she sensed a rejection coming.

It was a new feeling for her as she was used to being the one to say no. It was a new feeling for her as she'd always *wanted* to be the one to say no. It was a new feeling for her as she had never in her life been mad, crazy, hopelessly in love with the man who was about to be rent from her life.

It was a new feeling she didn't want to be feeling any more or ever again.

She braced herself as he opened his jacket to reveal another perfectly pressed shirt. His hand disappeared inside a pocket before coming back out wrapped around something.

He reached across to her and uncurled his fingers revealing a small velvet-covered box.

She stared at it for a few unseeing seconds before looking up into his eyes, which now were nowhere near as unreadable as they had been mere moments earlier.

The feverish look in his eyes *was* one she had seen before. It was the same look clients would get before sinking their entire life savings into a solitary baseball card in a great gamble that it would appreciate in years to come.

'It's for you,' he said.

She uncurled her white-knuckled fingers from the cane and slowly took the box from his hand. She let it rest in her lap for a few moments before opening it with a jerky click.

If she'd felt as if she were being flayed alive earlier, now she felt as though all the pieces of her that had been torn apart were scattering to the four winds with no possible hope of being put back together again.

Inside the old box was a ring. And not just any ring. His great-grandmother's ring. The one his mother had been so loath to let go at the auction. The one that had called to her way back then. The one that had been lovingly kept for Mitch Hanover to give to the woman he loved.

But the man holding it out to her now looked more as if he was about to jump off a cliff.

She looked up at him. 'What's this?'

His eyes flickered for a moment before he said, 'It's round, sparkly, about the size of your next-to-last finger. I have a feeling it's a ring.'

She didn't look away as she carefully said, 'Mitch, it's an engagement ring.'

When he didn't extrapolate further she was forced to ask, 'Are you asking me to marry you?'

'I am.'

'Why?'

'Why?' he coughed out. 'Because I want you to stay, that's why.'

'And where do you think I'm going?'

He shifted uncomfortably on the edge of the crackly seat. 'You do have a habit of not staying in one place for all that long. And every time I think of you leaving us in five months, I can't have it.'

She nodded. He liked having her around. She made him feel good. He wanted her to stay, not because he couldn't live without her, but for what she could do for him—make his life a little louder, a little brighter, a little more challenging than it had been before.

She was living a permanent *déjà vu*.

She closed her eyes tight. Because this time it didn't *feel* at all the same. This time her heart was so deeply involved it hurt. Because she loved this man. Truly, madly and deeply. And what he was offering her came not from the same place at all.

For him their affair had been about taking a much-needed step forward in his stagnant life. For her it had been about stepping into the light.

As though he sensed her dissatisfaction with his answer he cleared his throat, then added, 'But it's not just that.'

It's not? Her heart did its pitter-pat, thumpety-thump and added a little jig of hope.

'You have to admit we make one hell of a good team.'

A good team? *A good team?* Right. Right! With him being the captain and with her being the catcher of all his problems. The rubber of his feet after a long day at the office. The mopper of his brow as he woke from nightmares reliving the loss of the wife he'd truly loved.

Damn it. Damn *him* for being so stubborn and beautiful and irresistible to a girl who couldn't help but veer towards those who needed her most. Damn him for making her love him.

'Have you even heard a word I've ever said to you? No. You just don't listen!' she said so loudly he flinched. '*None* of you ever do.'

Mitch, the king of dry wit, looked over his shoulder as though expecting a gang lined up behind him. 'None of who?'

She glared at him with every fibre of her being. 'Men!'

'Men.'

She poked him in the chest, her finger coming into contact with a wall of gorgeous suit and just as gorgeous hard muscle. She knew. She'd seen it up close and personal. Run her fingers along it, savouring every ridge and valley. And she was now paying the price for it.

'I may seem the personification of fun and games to you. A bouncy little carefree chickadee. But it's an act. All of it. A way of covering up how much I want people to accept me. To need me. To appreciate how good I really am at what I do. Of covering up that I so want to put down roots in my life but am terrified that I'll get too attached before being uprooted all over again. And that if I bounce around like none of it matters, then the day that I have to leave, as because of you men I always end up having to leave, it won't hurt so much to do so.'

'Who said anything about leaving? Veronica, I want you to stay. For ever.'

She saw him swallow before he said the words. He wasn't any more in love with her than Geoffrey had been.

Her heart broke. It felt just as if he'd pressed his finger to the side of an antique ceramic jar and pushed.

'So draw up a new contract,' she said.

'That's what I'm trying to do here.'

She reached out her hand, palm up, and offered him back the ring.

He stared at her hand for a few moments. Finally, when he looked back into her eyes, she could have sworn she saw a reflection of her own feelings therein, a depth and import and honesty that gripped her struggling heart like a vice as a shot of quicksilver emotion shone from inside him like a beacon.

But it was gone before she could take it to heart.

'You can't deny how amazing we are together.'

'Yet you don't love me, Mitch. You loved Claire. You love your family. You love your business. I even think you've come to love playing the part of the wounded widower for the relief it gives you. I can't compete with that and I wouldn't want to.'

His eyes flashed with emotion as he reached out to take the ring and she thought she might have got out of this lightly. But then he snatched his empty hand back and stood, pacing to the edge of the concrete where he looked out across the road to St Kilda Beach.

'You're wrong,' he said, his voice terse.

'I'm not.'

He turned, looking her in the eye with such intimate intensity her heart leapt so high she had to slap it back down.

'I may have been that way once. But not anymore. I've changed. You changed me. And I don't want to change back.'

Of all the words he could have chosen to reel her in…

But no. She'd come too far to accept being second-best, to care for a man who needed looking after in a way she simply couldn't do unless he gave her the exact same amount of care in return. Their relationship would never be balanced and she couldn't do that to herself. She wouldn't. She mustn't. Or she'd only come to blame him for it in the end.

'Fine,' she said, her voice cooler than she felt. 'Then tell me you love me.'

'Tell me you don't love me,' he shot back.

She sprung to her feet and then turned and headed for the stairs. He caught up to her before she made it, grabbing her by the upper arm and whirling her back to face him.

'Let me go, Mitch.'

'I can't,' he said.

The way he said it felt as if he meant it. As if he simply couldn't bear to let her go. But he hadn't been able to summon the words she needed to hear.

'You can,' she said.

'Only if you'll stay and talk to me.'

She wondered if bending her arm back and giving him the slip might be the better choice, but she'd left her shoes and apartment keys back on the sun lounger.

'Fine,' she said. 'I'll stay. So long as you keep a distance of two metres at any given time.'

'I've never met someone so intent on setting so many rules for themselves.'

'Look in the mirror.'

His gaze softened, her heart skipped and danced, and she did bend her arm away, not wanting to see what might happen if he kept a hold of her.

'Two metres,' she said.

He backed away, arms raised. 'Deal.'

His choice of words was not helpful considering the topic of conversation.

He moved to take up position resting his backside against a patch of the concrete balustrade. He crossed his feet at the ankles and his arms across his chest. 'Are you really rejecting my proposal?'

She could have pointed out that it hadn't been a proposal so much as the shoving of a ring at a girl expecting her to figure it out, but instead she went with, 'I have no interest in being anybody's wife.'

'Why not?'

'Because after spending the best years of my life taking care of other people, I was left alone. Devastated. It took time to find my feet. And now that I have, this time is my time for me. I will not be anybody's nursemaid.'

'I don't need a nursemaid.'

'Are you sure about that?'

His cheek twitched and she almost leapt across the divide so that she could kiss the spot before it faded.

But for the first time in a long time she was being good. She was taking care of herself. It was the hardest thing she'd ever had to do, but she knew that if she was finally going to take the last step into adulthood, she had to do it now.

'Mitch, we should never have begun what we've begun. And I don't blame you, I really don't. It was all me. I knew better and I let it happen anyway. Heck, from the first time you smiled at me I practically begged for it to happen. But you don't want this. You don't want to marry me.'

'So now what?'

Oh, heavens, did she have to say it? She had been avoiding even thinking about the ramifications of his declaration, much less putting them into words.

'Now you turn around and go home. Tomorrow you go to work at your office, I go to work at mine. And the next time we see one another it will be as boss and employee and nothing else.'

'But I… You…'

His neck turned red as he struggled through a quagmire of practised emotional isolation for words that would not come. But that was the problem right there. The words came to her with such ease there was no mistaking the truth of them. But Mitch was fighting the words like a drowning man swimming against the tide.

'Go home, Mitch. Have a drink. Put your feet up. Give yourself a half an hour and you'll realise you've been given a second chance. And if we can both be grown up about this, then I don't see why we can't move past this hiccup and have a perfectly nice working relationship.'

He pushed himself away from the balustrade. Storm clouds gathered in his eyes. Her yearning, loving, overwrought heart reached out to him, and her feet were so close to following she had to dig her toes into the concrete.

'Go home, Mitch,' she repeated, this time with an insistence she didn't feel.

His eyes narrowed. He looked as if he had more he wanted to say. She silently begged him to push through and walk to her and gather her in his arms and profess his undying love for her, and to promise to take care of her for the rest of her life.

But his eyes eventually settled back to their usual impenetrable grey. He nodded. Just the once. Then walked by.

Veronica watched his back, the dark suit, the neat hair, the shoulders that were perfectly broad enough for her to lean on.

He'd offered them to her for ever and she was about to let them go.

The words '*Mitch, wait*,' stung the back of her throat, but by the time they made it to the tip of her tongue he was down the stairs and out of sight.

She and her shaky legs made it back to the cane lounger seconds before her knees gave way. She dropped her head into her palms and let the shakes that had been coming from the second she'd seen him on her rooftop take over her.

There was nothing she could do to quell them. Or the bone-deep ache. Or the mental scalding. Or the warm salty tears.

She loved him yet she'd had to let him go. And everyone at work would know. She'd said before a workplace like theirs was like a small town and she hadn't been exaggerating. The thought of Gretel and Boris and Smithy whispering behind her back hurt almost as much.

In the real world they could never go back to being merely boss and employee, not when she felt the way she did about him. There was no getting around it. She would have to go.

So much for never sacrificing her own happiness for others' ever again.

Maybe she'd been kidding herself all along. Maybe falling on her sword was to be the motif of her life. If it was she'd loved and lost and survived. She would simply have to do it again.

After a few wretched minutes she sniffed deep, wiped her tears and looked up into the beautiful blue sky that was now streaked with a horizon of clouds lit orange by the setting sun.

She let it soak into her, especially when it became clear that it would be the last Melbourne sunset she would see for some time.

It was dark by the time she got to her feet. Her legs were still shaky. Her eyes raw. But that was nothing compared with the heaviness in her chest when she gathered her things to find Mitch's great-grandmother's ring was still sitting atop her folded-up jacket.

She opened the velvet case, watched the diamonds sparkle hopefully in the low light. Then, before the history and meaning and possibility of the piece broke her into a million little pieces, she snapped it shut, wrapped it in her jacket and padded across the roof and down the stairs and into her apartment.

CHAPTER ELEVEN

THE next day Mitch sat at his office desk, staring out over the Melbourne skyline, which was as grey and clouded as his mood.

A knock came at his door. He checked his watch and spun his chair as the door swung inward. 'I said I didn't want to be disturbed for at least another three minutes,' he growled.

Kristin's dark head popped around the corner. 'It's Gretel on the phone.'

He continued shooting her a flat stare.

She merely rolled her eyes and said, 'From the gallery. She sounds pretty upset. And she would only talk to you.'

He glanced at the flashing red button on his phone. The gallery. Perhaps he could carefully wangle out of her how Veronica was this morning. If she perhaps looked anywhere near as bad as he did. If she'd slept as fitfully. If she'd regretted her words and actions on that rooftop as much as he had his. If they might still be able to take three steps back and simply slow things down and stay on the same path. He could only hope so.

'Are you gonna take it?' Kristin asked.

'I am.'

'Be nice.'

'I'm always nice.'

'Ha! Just be…less like you usually are, okay? She sounds fragile. And she does have a crush on you, you know.'

He waved Kristin away. She shot him a comparable hand gesture, which he only caught the back of, but by the time he opened his mouth to ask what she meant by it his door was closed.

He picked up the phone. 'Gretel, what can I do for you?'

Gretel sniffed and blew her nose before saying, 'I tried to call your mother but I only got the answer machine at home, and I didn't know who else to call. But she's gone.'

He didn't need to ask who. He sat forward in his chair so fast his knees hit wood beneath the desk. 'Gone where?'

'Gone gone. When she came into work this morning she gathered us all together and sat us down to tell us she was leaving.'

That got him to his feet. *'Leaving?'*

'For good. She said she'd already e-mailed you her resignation and that she had to go today.'

He quickly opened his e-mail and found hers among about twenty others from members of his staff sending him tedious spreadsheets and profit-and-loss reports.

His eyes ran briskly over the short but firm letter, which thanked him for the opportunity, apologised that the job had not been what she'd hoped it might be and requested that he not pay her for the week gone in recompense for the short notice.

He was losing her. He was really and truly losing her. Her energy, her vibrancy, the spark that she lit inside him. Her bright ideas and raucous laugh. Her enthusiasm for his family and his family business. Her talent, her beauty, her kindness. Even her friendship.

He imagined what it would feel like to wake up the next day and feel her gone, heading out of town like a westerly wind.

He swore beneath his breath, shoved his phone beneath his

ear, grabbed his jacket from over the back of his chair and shucked it on one-handed.

'When did she leave, Gretel?'

'Just now. She looked awful. Wretched. Not at all like the Veronica we all know and love. What did you do to her?'

'Me?' he asked, his voice rising in surprise. And since when had everyone in his life taken it upon themselves to think they could boss him around? First Kristin, then his mother, now mousy little Gretel?

Oh, he knew when. Since Veronica had come into their lives and taught them chutzpah, that was when.

He let his voice drop several notes when he demanded, 'Where did she say she was going, Gretel?'

Her silence was stubborn.

'Gretel, if you want her back, then you're going to have to tell me.'

She gave a dramatic little sigh before saying, 'She'd left something behind at home and is coming back later to drop it off. She said she'd be back in the next half an hour or so. After that I have no idea. Whatever you did, fix it, Mr Hanover, please. We love her—we don't want her to go. Without her everything's just going to go back to the way it was. And none of us want that.'

He gripped the phone so tight his fingers hurt. *Back to the way it was.* Gretel was right. None of them wanted that.

Things had changed, and only for the better. For things to continue to change he needed Veronica. They all needed Veronica. They loved her. He loved her.

He loved her. There was not a lick of doubt in his mind. Now he only needed to make her believe it too.

'Gretel, I'm on my way over. If she gets there before me, stall her.'

Gretel sniffed one last time and he could almost imagine her drawing herself up to her full five feet. 'Yes, Mr Hanover. I won't let her go.'

Twenty-seven minutes later Mitch pulled up outside Hanover House. It didn't occur to him to care that he'd parked in the no-parking zone.

He shot from his car, turned his hand in its general direction and pressed the remote lock without checking if it had worked, then burst through the front door.

Gretel was behind the reception desk with a customer. As soon as she saw him, she flapped a manic hand towards the back of the gallery. He gave a momentary double take at the new pink stripes in her hair before jogging up the stairs three at a time.

Eyes whipping from one side of the gallery to the other and not seeing her, he kept going until he reached the back office. The door was ajar, he stepped inside, and his relief was so strong he felt it slide through his body like liquid heat as he saw she was still there.

She was bent from the waist with her gorgeous backside facing towards him. Head down, dark curls hanging until they almost touched the ground, she wore the same jeans she had the first day he'd met her, though in place of a black sleeveless T-shirt and knee-high boots she wore a stylish tailored navy velvet jacket and beaded beige heels he was certain he'd seen in the store in town where he normally bought his own work shoes.

It seemed she'd not only rubbed off on him, he'd rubbed off on her somewhat, as well. It gave him one hell of a burst of hope.

As she righted herself she must have sensed his presence as she said, 'Oh, Gretel, honey, have you seen my red suede boots? I think I—'

Her words came to a halt when she saw that he was not, in fact, Gretel.

'Don't stop on my account,' he said. 'You think you…'

As she looked right through him as if he were some kind of apparition her brown eyes were large and luminous in a face he had never seen so pale. He'd been hoping she'd had as bad a night as he had, but now he saw that she had he took it all back. Her pain only doubled his own. It was enough to solidify his resolve to do whatever he had to do to clean up the god-awful mess he'd made.

He'd been arrogant. He'd handled himself like an oaf. But that was what came from not having to truly woo a woman for almost ten years. But nobody got to where he had without skills. No matter what Veronica Bing thought, when it was needed, he could sell himself with the best of them.

'Your red suede boots,' he prompted.

She swallowed before saying, 'I think I left them behind when I got changed here before the auction.'

'And you needed them so desperately right this minute because…'

She straightened her shoulders, the velvet jacket sliding to curve around her hips just so. 'Because I'm leaving. Didn't you get my e-mail?'

'I got it. I just wanted to hear you tell me so to my face.'

'So that's why you're here?'

He moved into the room. 'That's one of the reasons. One I'd like to sort out before moving on to the others. I'm sorry, but I won't accept your resignation.'

If she'd looked dejected before, now she looked like a puppy caught out in the rain. He ached to reach for her, to hug away her sorrow, but he couldn't. Not yet. They had issues to sort through before he could allow things to turn physical. He'd tried

showing her how he felt that way before but she was so mulish
and it had obviously not been enough.

'We have a contract,' he said.

'So sue me.' She shrugged and it seemed to expel about as
much energy as she could muster.

He took a seat on the corner of the desk, bringing his eyes
level with hers. Her great big pools of burnished bronze looking back at him as though begging him to put her out of her
misery.

'I thought you liked it here,' he said, his voice gentle, encouraging.

She gulped. 'I did. I do. I love it. It's the best job I've ever
had.'

'Then why leave?'

She blinked and a modicum of her usual bravado returned.
'It's a staffing issue.'

He crossed his arms. 'Tell me who's giving you grief and
I'll fire them instead.'

One hand moved to land upon her hip as she jutted it sideways. *Oh, yeah, there's the girl I know and love*, he thought.
But after that admission he could think no further.

He did love her. Honestly. Truly. Altogether. How could he
not? To know Veronica was to love her. It really was that simple. And for a guy who liked things simple it boosted his confidence tenfold.

'Don't be fractious,' she said. 'You know perfectly well I
mean you. I can't work with you. Not now. Not after last night.
And not after the days and nights before that, either. It's been
a right royal mess from the very beginning. Therefore, as
always, I have to be the one to leave. Though, if you would
kindly step down from the head of Hanover Enterprises, or
better yet, sell Hanover House, then perhaps I'll reconsider.'

'Fine,' he said. 'If you want this place, it's yours.'

She raised her right hand to her chest. 'What do you mean mine?'

She looked so adorably confused he couldn't stand it any longer. He lifted himself from the desk and walked over to take her hand in his.

'Veronica, for such a smart, sensitive, shrewd woman I wonder how it is that you can't see the most important things that are right under your nose.'

Her hand curled ever so lightly around his and it gave him a shot of hope so strong he almost felt himself levitate. But this wasn't a settled thing yet. Not by a long shot. He dug his heels hard into the ground.

'I proposed to you last night. Knowing me as you do, do you really believe that is something I would ever take lightly?'

She blinked, her wide brown eyes not leaving his for a second. Then after a few moments in which he thought she might argue back just because she couldn't help herself, she shook her head.

'Good. Because I've only been in love twice in my life. Once to a woman who I thought was going to be my partner for the rest of my life. It took some time to come to terms with that not being the case. I hit rock-bottom, working insane hours, cutting myself off from anyone who might show me a way through. And then you walked through my door.'

He reached out and cupped her chin with his palm. She sank against it and he knew then that he hadn't been wrong. Not wrong to hire her, not wrong to give her free rein to be herself, not wrong to love her, and not wrong to open himself up to the pain of losing her if it gave him one last chance to keep her in his life.

'You,' he continued. 'Bright, bubbly, smart, excessive, argumentative, difficult, gorgeous, sexy you. You were the last thing

I thought I wanted in my life, but it turns out you are exactly what I need. What I desire. What I now won't let go without a fight. And if that means giving up the family business to you and your band of merry no-hopers to turn the place into a rotating circus populated by mad local artisans who would send old Phineas Hanover turning in his grave, then that's what I'm willing to do.'

'But your parents—' she said, before his thumb running over her bottom lip cut her off.

'Adore you.'

'But Claire—'

'Was a huge part of my life. Was the first woman I ever loved. But as it turns out, she is not the last.'

When he looked back into her eyes, they were rimmed with tears. Her nostrils were flaring and her bottom lip had begun to quiver. Her excess of emotion reached out and circled him, drawing him in, making him want her, and desire her and need her more and more every second he was in her company.

'Any more buts?'

She thought about it. He saw the wheels spinning behind her eyes as she searched high and low for another reason why this couldn't be happening to her. And he didn't blame her—he'd felt the same way for the past three weeks himself.

'What are you so afraid of?' he asked, tucking a stray curl behind her ear.

'I thought you were certain I was Captain Fearless.'

'On many levels you are. But right now I can feel you quivering.'

'I'm sensitive to the cold, remember?' she said.

'Rubbish. You're terrified.'

'Of what?'

'Of actually walking out that door and leaving this place. Of leaving Gretel and Boris. Or leaving me. I know this because I can see myself in your eyes. I've been afraid of so many things for such a long time. Of seeing my father deteriorate. Watching my mother fear for the life of the business which she holds so close to her heart. Of getting close to someone again. But now, right this second, I am completely without fear.'

'Then whatever's making you feel that way you should bottle it.'

Mitch laughed. From the bottom of his gut he laughed. 'Nah,' he said, 'I plan on keeping that secret all to myself. So.'

'So,' she said, still doing her best to keep her cool, as though she still couldn't make herself believe what was happening. The time had come to stop prepping her, to stop laying down the cotton wool and let her fall right along with him.

'Veronica.'

'Yes, Mitch.'

'I want you to stay. I want you to marry me. I want to love you. Now that I know I want to be with you for ever, I don't want to waste another second of it. You said it once—life's short. You've gotta live it. And I want to live mine with you.'

This time as he said the words aloud he felt them from the bottom of his heart.

He saw that she knew he meant it too. Her eyes turned soft, her lips went lax, and as though she'd merely been waiting for the magic words she leant in and placed a gentle, warm, mes-merising kiss upon his lips.

When she pulled away, she said, 'I'm in love with you too, Mitch Hanover. Have been for as long as I can remember. I'm fairly certain it started before I even met you. Some time around my eighth birthday when I got my first Ken doll for my Barbie to marry.'

'Then I guess I have some catching up to do.'

She laughed and ran a quick finger beneath her left eye before a tear managed to spill, and it was then that he noticed the sparkle from her left ring finger.

Her eyes opened wide as she saw the direction of his gaze. He reached out and grabbed her hand before she had the chance to snatch it away.

She was wearing his great-grandmother's ring.

He held her hand out flat, staring at the familiar thin band and small diamond setting. It looked so at home on her long thin fingers, which felt warm in his own. Warm and ever so slightly shaking.

She gave a pathetic little shrug as she said, 'I forgot to bring it when I came in this morning. Then when I got here I just wanted to try it on once before I left it behind for you. And then I couldn't get it off. I've tried everything. Soap, glycerine, tugging. But it only made my knuckle swell up. And now it's stuck.'

At that he more than laughed, he cracked. Waves and waves of rollicking laughter swept through him as he realised all his pretty speeches had been for nothing. She was his and had been all along.

'It's not funny,' she said, though for the first time that morning she began to crack a smile. The quivering had stopped and her warmth and energy had pushed through some kind of barrier until his Veronica was back. 'I seriously can't get it off.'

'So don't take it off.'

She snapped her mouth shut. But the smile remained. 'Your great-grandmother had tiny fingers. If I don't take it off my ring finger will soon turn purple and fall off.'

'Come here.' He slowly slid an arm about her waist pulling her to him, and she didn't resist in the slightest. In fact, she melted against him so readily if the door hadn't been open he might well have cleared the desk with a swipe of his arm and taken her then and there.

Instead he found her hand again, put the ring finger in his mouth, swirled his tongue around the edges, then, using his teeth, he gently coaxed the ring from her finger into his mouth. He then grinned at her with the ring sticking out from between his teeth.

'Marry me,' he said.

She leant in and kissed him again, this time sliding her tongue into his mouth to tease him, to frustrate him, to show him how she felt and to take the ring back.

When they pulled apart she let the ring plop onto her palm, looked up at him with love pouring from her bright brown eyes, and said, 'You bet I will.'

A commotion erupted outside the office and they both turned as Miriam came rushing in, her usual loose suit flapping about her legs. 'But I heard she was gone. What happened? What did he do?'

Boris and Gretel followed hot on her heels. And Kristin brought up the rear. Like a four-car pile-up they came to a halt in the doorway when they spotted the two of them entwined around one another.

'Oh,' Miriam said. 'Boris called Gerald, who rang me on my mobile, and I of course checked with Kristin and we all came down here and here you are.'

'It doesn't look as if they're fighting,' Boris said.

'Not any fighting I've ever done,' Gretel said.

Veronica waggled the ring at Miriam, who understood in a split second, rushing to her and enveloping her in a bear hug.

Kristin threw her hands in the air. 'Will someone please tell me what's going on?'

'Your mad friend has just agreed to marry me,' Mitch said, his voice as dry as sandpaper. Nevertheless Kristin got into the spirit and threw herself into his arms.

Boris and Gretel hugged whoever they could just to feel part of the action.

Mitch did his best to disentangle the limbs strangling him and keeping him separated from the one person he wanted to have his arms around in that moment. 'Right. Everyone, this has been fun, but will you please now all get out?'

He used his best boss voice. Yet they all blinked back at him. And he knew then that the time had passed when they were all so afraid of him they'd simply do as they were told.

So he turned Kristin on the spot, gave her a shove, pushing the others in her wake, and he shut the door behind them.

He leant against the door for fear of a reprise. 'My life held not nearly so much excitement before you came along, Ms Bing.'

She sauntered over to him, her sexy hips swinging to and fro. 'You'd better get used to it, Mr Hanover. It kind of follows me through life like flotsam and jetsam.'

She leant bodily against him and ran her finger beneath his chin, scraping along his stubble. 'So the Hanover House deal. Are you really going to give it to me?'

'Nah,' he said, just about managing to keep his wits, 'that was all part of my grand sales pitch, therefore nought but smoke and mirrors. Giving the customer what she believes she wants in order to get what I want. Isn't that how it works?'

Her eyes widened. 'Wow. I never knew you had it in you.'

'I've learned from the best.'

'Mmm. Though it would make a nice wedding present.'

'What's mine will already be yours.'

'True, but I am my own woman, after all.'

He gave in and enfolded her in his arms, so close her knee slid between his thighs and their noses touched.

'Not anymore,' he said. 'You're my woman now.'

And with that he kissed her, deeply, letting go completely, showing her just how much he loved her and cared for her.

And Mitch let Veronica's warmth soak deep inside him until he couldn't remember a time when he hadn't felt this happy.

* * * * *

Coming next month in
M&B Modern Extra Romance August 2008:

PREGNANT BY THE PLAYBOY TYCOON
by Anne Oliver

Anneliese is trying to rebuild herself and find her true family—but one man keeps getting in her way. Gorgeous businessman Steve Anderson feels duty-bound to protect his sister's best friend, even if she has got her frosty barriers in place. And then he finds Annie's deep freeze is on fast thaw...

HOUSEFEEPER AT HIS BECK AND CALL
by Susan Stephens

Lieutenant Cade Grant is rugged, strong and gorgeous, but his heart is as hard as they come. Sweet, innocent, and in need of employment *fast*, Liv will do almost anything. If that means donning her housekeeper's pinny for the brooding lieutenant, then so be it. But the job description has been changed—the situation vacant is now in his bed!

MILLS & BOON®
Pure reading pleasure™

AUGUST 2008 HARDBACK TITLES

ROMANCE

Virgin for the Billionaire's Taking	978 0 263 20334 9
Penny Jordan	
Purchased: His Perfect Wife *Helen Bianchin*	978 0 263 20335 6
The Vasquez Mistress *Sarah Morgan*	978 0 263 20336 3
At the Sheikh's Bidding *Chantelle Shaw*	978 0 263 20337 0
The Spaniard's Marriage Bargain *Abby Green*	978 0 263 20338 7
Sicilian Millionaire, Bought Bride	978 0 263 20339 4
Catherine Spencer	
Italian Prince, Wedlocked Wife *Jennie Lucas*	978 0 263 20340 0
The Desert King's Pregnant Bride *Annie West*	978 0 263 20341 7
Bride at Briar's Ridge *Margaret Way*	978 0 263 20342 4
Last-Minute Proposal *Jessica Hart*	978 0 263 20343 1
The Single Mum and the Tycoon	978 0 263 20344 8
Caroline Anderson	
Found: His Royal Baby *Raye Morgan*	978 0 263 20345 5
The Millionaire's Nanny Arrangement	978 0 263 20346 2
Linda Goodnight	
Hired: The Boss's Bride *Ally Blake*	978 0 263 20347 9
A Boss Beyond Compare *Dianne Drake*	978 0 263 20348 6
The Emergency Doctor's Chosen Wife	978 0 263 20349 3
Molly Evans	

HISTORICAL

Scandalising the Ton *Diane Gaston*	978 0 263 20207 6
Her Cinderella Season *Deb Marlowe*	978 0 263 20208 3
The Warrior's Princess Bride *Meriel Fuller*	978 0 263 20209 0

MEDICAL™

A Baby for Eve *Maggie Kingsley*	978 0 263 19906 2
Marrying the Millionaire Doctor *Alison Roberts*	978 0 263 19907 9
His Very Special Bride *Joanna Neil*	978 0 263 19908 6
City Surgeon, Outback Bride *Lucy Clark*	978 0 263 19909 3

⬤ MILLS & BOON®
Pure reading pleasure™

AUGUST 2008 LARGE PRINT TITLES

ROMANCE

The Italian Billionaire's Pregnant Bride *Lynne Graham*	978 0 263 20066 9
The Guardian's Forbidden Mistress *Miranda Lee*	978 0 263 20067 6
Secret Baby, Convenient Wife *Kim Lawrence*	978 0 263 20068 3
Caretti's Forced Bride *Jennie Lucas*	978 0 263 20069 0
The Bride's Baby *Liz Fielding*	978 0 263 20070 6
Expecting a Miracle *Jackie Braun*	978 0 263 20071 3
Wedding Bells at Wandering Creek *Patricia Thayer*	978 0 263 20072 0
The Loner's Guarded Heart *Michelle Douglas*	978 0 263 20073 7

HISTORICAL

Lady Gwendolen Investigates *Anne Ashley*	978 0 263 20163 5
The Unknown Heir *Anne Herries*	978 0 263 20164 2
Forbidden Lord *Helen Dickson*	978 0 263 20165 9

MEDICAL™

The Doctor's Bride By Sunrise *Josie Metcalfe*	978 0 263 19968 0
Found: A Father For Her Child *Amy Andrews*	978 0 263 19969 7
A Single Dad at Heathermere *Abigail Gordon*	978 0 263 19970 3
Her Very Special Baby *Lucy Clark*	978 0 263 19971 0
The Heart Surgeon's Secret Son *Janice Lynn*	978 0 263 19972 7
The Sheikh Surgeon's Proposal *Olivia Gates*	978 0 263 19973 4

MILLS & BOON
Pure reading pleasure

SEPTEMBER 2008 HARDBACK TITLES

ROMANCE

Ruthlessly Bedded by the Italian Billionaire *Emma Darcy*	978 0 263 20350 9
Mendez's Mistress *Anne Mather*	978 0 263 20351 6
Rafael's Suitable Bride *Cathy Williams*	978 0 263 20352 3
Desert Prince, Defiant Virgin *Kim Lawrence*	978 0 263 20353 0
Sicilian Husband, Unexpected Baby *Sharon Kendrick*	978 0 263 20354 7
Hired: The Italian's Convenient Mistress *Carol Marinelli*	978 0 263 20355 4
Antonides' Forbidden Wife *Anne McAllister*	978 0 263 20356 1
The Millionaire's Chosen Bride *Susanne James*	978 0 263 20357 8
Wedded in a Whirlwind *Liz Fielding*	978 0 263 20358 5
Blind Date with the Boss *Barbara Hannay*	978 0 263 20359 2
The Tycoon's Christmas Proposal *Jackie Braun*	978 0 263 20360 8
Christmas Wishes, Mistletoe Kisses *Fiona Harper*	978 0 263 20361 5
Rescued by the Magic of Christmas *Melissa McClone*	978 0 263 20362 2
Her Millionaire, His Miracle *Myrna Mackenzie*	978 0 263 20363 9
Italian Doctor, Sleigh-Bell Bride *Sarah Morgan*	978 0 263 20364 6
The Desert Surgeon's Secret Son *Olivia Gates*	978 0 263 20365 3

HISTORICAL

Scandalous Secret, Defiant Bride *Helen Dickson*	978 0 263 20210 6
A Question of Impropriety *Michelle Styles*	978 0 263 20211 3
Conquering Knight, Captive Lady *Anne O'Brien*	978 0 263 20212 0

MEDICAL™

Dr Devereux's Proposal *Margaret McDonagh*	978 0 263 19910 9
Children's Doctor, Meant-to-be Wife *Meredith Webber*	978 0 263 19911 6
Christmas at Willowmere *Abigail Gordon*	978 0 263 19912 3
Dr Romano's Christmas Baby *Amy Andrews*	978 0 263 19913 0

MILLS & BOON®

Pure reading pleasure™

SEPTEMBER 2008 LARGE PRINT TITLES

ROMANCE

The Markonos Bride *Michelle Reid*	978 0 263 20074 4
The Italian's Passionate Revenge *Lucy Gordon*	978 0 263 20075 1
The Greek Tycoon's Baby Bargain *Sharon Kendrick*	978 0 263 20076 8
Di Cesare's Pregnant Mistress *Chantelle Shaw*	978 0 263 20077 5
His Pregnant Housekeeper *Caroline Anderson*	978 0 263 20078 2
The Italian Playboy's Secret Son *Rebecca Winters*	978 0 263 20079 9
Her Sheikh Boss *Carol Grace*	978 0 263 20080 5
Wanted: White Wedding *Natasha Oakley*	978 0 263 20081 2

HISTORICAL

The Last Rake In London *Nicola Cornick*	978 0 263 20166 6
The Outrageous Lady Felsham *Louise Allen*	978 0 263 20167 3
An Unconventional Miss *Dorothy Elbury*	978 0 263 20168 0

MEDICAL™

The Surgeon's Fatherhood Surprise *Jennifer Taylor*	978 0 263 19974 1
The Italian Surgeon Claims His Bride *Alison Roberts*	978 0 263 19975 8
Desert Doctor, Secret Sheikh *Meredith Webber*	978 0 263 19976 5
A Wedding in Warragurra *Fiona Lowe*	978 0 263 19977 2
The Firefighter and the Single Mum *Laura Iding*	978 0 263 19978 9
The Nurse's Little Miracle *Molly Evans*	978 0 263 19979 6